"Get down!"

Colt dove on top of her.

Crack!

Colt calculated the risk of running back to the house, which was about a mile from here, or hauling it deeper into the woods. The sniper likely had a scope, which made them toast in the open. His only option was taking Georgia into the forest for cover.

"This way," he urged and pointed her into the woods, shielding her from behind.

They were dealing with an experienced shooter. His heart pounded but he kept a cool head as his training kicked into high gear. Nothing mattered more than Georgia's protection. He yanked her behind a massive oak tree.

"Stay low." Crouching, he hovered over Georgia as he used the trees as shields while maneuvering them farther into the woods. Leaves crunched underfoot, twigs snapped and the dogs barked, which would easily give away their position.

Suddenly, Georgia froze. Sweat poured down her pasty white cheeks. "I—I can't."

"Can't what?" Was she sick? What was happening?

Her breathing became shallow. "I'm—I'm having a panic attack."

Jessica R. Patch lives in the Mid-South, where she pens inspirational contemporary romance and romantic suspense novels. When she's not hunched over her laptop or going on adventurous trips with willing friends in the name of research, you can find her watching way too much Netflix with her family and collecting recipes for amazing dishes she'll probably never cook. To learn more about Jessica, please visit her at jessicarpatch.com.

Visit the Author Profile page at Harlequin.com for more titles.

COLD CASE TAKEDOWN

JESSICA R. PATCH

LOVE INSPIRED SUSPENSE

INSPIRATIONAL ROMANCE

LOVE INSPIRED® SUSPENSE
INSPIRATIONAL ROMANCE

Recycling programs
for this product may
not exist in your area.

ISBN-13: 978-1-335-40515-9

Cold Case Takedown

Love Inspired
22 Adelaide St. West, 40th Floor
Toronto, Ontario M5H 4E3, Canada
www.Harlequin.com

Printed in U.S.A.

And he said unto me, My grace is sufficient for thee:
for my strength is made perfect in weakness.
Most gladly therefore will I rather glory in my infirmities,
that the power of Christ may rest upon me.
—2 Corinthians 12:9

To those who suffer from anxiety and panic attacks. May the grace of God be with you. You are strong and brave. Keep fighting and moving forward.

Thank you to everyone who helped to make this book be everything it was meant to be.

Rachel Kent: An author couldn't have asked for a better agent and encourager.

Shana Asaro: An author couldn't ask for a better editor!

Jodie Bailey: Thank you for sharing your story with me. You're a wonderful friend and author.

Susan Tuttle: Your brainstorming, ideas and insight always help me see the big picture.

ONE

Agent Colt McCoy had half a mind to turn his old Ford truck around right now, but he'd already come this far on Highway 8. No turning back. He rolled the windows down and let the crisp October gusts sweep in to cool his nerves.

He should have known before tonight that the host of the popular *Dead Talk* podcast was none other than Georgia Maxwell. Should've picked up on her inflections, insight and humor. Every Thursday night for months, he'd been tuning in to the armchair detective Christi Cold as she laid out cold cases. She had a love for mysteries, like Colt. Going into law enforcement would have seemed like the logical first choice for his career, not football, but it was his best friend Jared Toledo's death that had changed Colt's course.

His old man had hammered into Colt on a daily basis—and repeatedly if he'd been drinking—that he was going to amount to absolutely nothing.

Some days those words rang like truth, until he reminded himself that he was the unit chief for the Mississippi Bureau of Investigation cold case unit. And in six weeks he was moving to Atlanta to accept a prestigious position overseeing the largest cold case squad in the South—minus the Texas Rangers unit. That would show his old man.

But even with the accolades and achievements, the haunted whispers of his insignificance and worthlessness sacked him at the fifty-yard line. He shoved away the rancid thoughts and turned up the podcast that had him driving almost an hour on his own time. It had gone live last night, and Colt had been awaiting the sharp thoughts of Christi Cold, aka Georgia.

He hadn't seen Georgia or been home in forever. It was the kind of place pictured in movies that women went gaga over during Christmas time—the ones that always ended with a happily-ever-after and the hometown boy winning the girl's heart.

Colt had almost had that story. Until Georgia had rejected him after graduation. Dad always said she was too good for a boy like Colt, that one day she'd wise up and run out on him like Mom had.

Dad had been right.

He shook out of the memories and listened to the host of the show in a new light and with a new voice—Georgia's.

Colt's cop radar had gone to wailing last night during the podcast. The case had been eerily similar to Jared's murder case. His gut had nagged him all day until he had made the quick decision to have his analyst get him the address for the host, whom he now knew to be Georgia. Which meant the case was definitely about Jared, though she'd used fictitious names, as she did with most of her cold cases. According to the podcast, Georgia had gained some insight from information she'd garnered that could possibly allow him to reopen the case.

He turned up the volume and listened.

"My interviews with former classmates and closest friends of Johnny Toliver..."

She was fudging or using old resources. Colt was Jared's best bud and he hadn't received a recent call from her.

"...all said he carried large amounts of cash and had expensive concert tickets in his possession. Front row. Pricey, friends. Pricey. Not that Johnny didn't come from a wealthy family—he did. But he rarely had that kind of money on his person. What I want to know is how he got it. I'll tell you how—in my opinion. I've discovered valid information that points to illegal athletic recruiting going on in one of Mississippi's finest high schools. I admit I haven't been able to put it all together as of yet, but I intend to, and if it pans out, I'll follow up with a sequel podcast. It's possible Johnny was approached and offered a nice, fat cash settlement and maybe even those concert tickets if he signed with the prestigious Ole Magnolia University."

This recruiting angle had never been investigated. The case had gone cold fast. Most everyone on their old Cougars football team suspected the QB from rival Southern High—Chance Leeway—as the murderer, which Georgia had noted with an alias name. Chance had made threats after a game. But he'd alibied out.

How did Georgia discover this new information? As far as Colt was aware, Georgia was not on any police force, but she had always dreamed of being a big-shot investigative journalist. Maybe she was. Colt had never kept tabs on her. It hurt too much.

"I suspect Johnny got cold feet, though. An upstanding young man known for his integrity and strong faith,

he may have succumbed to temptation, but the conviction weighed heavy on his heart. If he tried to give back the money, not attend Ole Magnolia on a full athletic scholarship and report the illegal recruiting, then more than one person had motive to kill him. I believe it could have been the high school coach. Though the town thinks he's above reproach, I know for a fact he's not. It could have been the coach from Ole Magnolia, or even a booster at the high school or college level, and there are several prominent ones who had pull. Or maybe they were in on it together.

"I say let the dog hunt and see what tree he goes barking up. My mama used to tell me that time will lift the truth to the surface and it'll bob in the water of lies for all to see. It's only a matter of a time."

That statement should have rung his bells last night. Georgia had always quoted her mama's line about truth. It was one of the few things Georgia said she remembered her mama saying. He'd been so focused on his own thoughts she'd sparked from her armchair detective work that he'd missed that line.

Until now.

If Georgia was onto something, then she could be in danger and not even realize it.

"Would you rather die a violent death and have your killer brought to justice or die quickly and the murderer never be found?"

Georgia Maxwell snapped to attention and caught her colleague Susan Towers's mischievous gleam as a gust of wind caught the *Magnolia Gazette*'s wooden sign, the wrought iron squeaking. "You are morbid," Georgia said. "Why aren't you writing for the crime news?" Georgia had been working for the *Magnolia Gazette* for the past ten years, covering the classifieds as well as the investigative reporting. Though there wasn't much crime to report, and she wasn't complaining.

Susan feigned innocence. "What? It's a valid question. We both know you dabble in true crime." She was referencing Georgia's popular podcast, *Dead Talk*. Georgia had brought it to life a year ago thanks to her love of mystery, thirst for justice and interest in true crime. In the first six months, it had become the number one cold case podcast series, coming to fans live every Thursday evening at seven.

"Yeah, well, you're not supposed to know." Georgia frowned. "You're nosy." Susan had discovered a couple of her podcast notes in her desk drawer one afternoon. Georgia had never intended on telling anyone she was Christi Cold—her voice-modified alias. That would be sharing intimate information, and she preferred keeping people at a nice, safe distance.

"I'm nosy? You're the one with information that links an illegal athletic recruiting ring to Jared's murder fifteen years ago. Bold statement, *Christi*. Where'd you snoop to find that nugget?"

She didn't snoop, per se. She found it when she cleaned out Dandy Martin's desk after her tragic death four months ago. Georgia had tried to tell her not to go running off to Memphis to shop alone at the Wolfchase Mall. A string of carjackings had been reported on the news. Dandy had laughed and told her, *You gotta live, Georgia. See you on Monday. I'll be fine.*

But she hadn't been fine. She'd been the first of the carjacking victims to be murdered.

Georgia might not be living her best life, but she

was alive. Too many people she'd cared about had been ripped from her thanks to an unsafe world.

Susan followed her gaze to Dandy's desk and clearly put the pieces together. "Dandy had investigative news?"

Georgia nodded.

"How did she get onto a story like that? Did it lead to Jared?"

Fifteen years ago, the case had been all over the news, the town. The state. Blunt-force trauma to the back of Jared's head. Killed in one location—which they never determined—and relocated to the athletic training room at Courage High. *Go Cougars.*

Georgia peeked at her two Shetland sheepdogs napping at her feet. Wyatt and Doc were her little companions. She called them therapy dogs, which was her way of justifying her attachment to the fur balls. A year ago, when Grandma had passed away, Georgia spiraled into a colossal meltdown. Didn't even leave her house for an entire month out of paralyzing fear. Dandy had recommended she see a Christian counselor.

She'd been seeing Celeste ever since, and she'd agreed the dogs were good for Georgia.

Finally, Georgia felt like she had answers to problems that had made her feel as if something was wrong with her all her life. No longer was she simply "Georgia the worrywart." The diagnosis of anxiety with panic disorder hadn't labeled her so much as helped her pinpoint the reason for her extreme fear and worry. She now had a ball to tackle and a field to run it down for the touchdown—mental health and freedom. Every day she picked it up and used her coping skills and prayer to make it another yard.

Some days were better than others.

She hadn't forfeited her prayer for complete healing. That was an everyday prayer. And each day the same Scripture whispered to her heart: "And He said unto me, My grace is sufficient for thee: for My strength is made perfect in weakness. Most gladly therefore will I rather glory in my infirmities, that the power of Christ may rest upon me."

Not the answer she wanted to hear, if truth be told, but she was learning to lean into grace in ways she never had before.

Susan snapped her fingers. "I asked how she got ahold of the story."

"Sorry. She got a letter from an anonymous parent after covering a school board meeting. Apparently, they were voting on students who moved school districts but had requested to stay at Courage High for the remainder of their school careers. One of the freshman students who played in the band was denied, but another freshman who played football for Coach Flanigan was granted permission to remain. The letter stated that they knew of a football student using a false address at 4214 Pine Road here in Magnolia and no one was saying a word about it, but to go check it out."

"Did she?"

Georgia nodded. "Dandy's notes confirm that 4214 Pine Road is nothing but a mailbox with the address numbers sitting on fourteen acres of woods." What were the kids doing? Pitching tents and bathing in a creek? No. It was a lie.

"Wow." Susan frowned. "Athletes always have been able to break rules. At least around here."

"For real. All I have are Dandy's beginning stages of notes. Two players are currently using the same address but live in other school districts." If Dandy had come to her, she could have already looked into it. She was the investigative reporter.

Susan unwrapped a green apple Jolly Rancher and winced as if she hadn't been expecting the tart flavor. "How did you come up with the illegal recruiting ring?"

"Dandy did. She had a list of students from years past who had also used the Pine Road address but lived in other districts. Those students then went on to receive full athletic scholarships to Ole Magnolia University. In another column, she had a list of students who literally moved from the Southern High school district to Courage High's district to play football, and those kids also went on to receive full rides at Ole Magnolia."

"Okay, so? Coach produces. He's only lost two state championships in the twenty-five years that he's coached. If I knew my kid had a better shot at a full ride to college, I'd move, too."

"I agree. But falsifying addresses sends up a red flag. It proves something deceptive is happening. Some of her scribbled questions and notes made sense. I decided to look into it myself. Guess what I found out?"

"What?"

"Five years ago, Coach moved from a modest home, what he could afford on a teacher's salary, to a big fat-daddy place on Knob Hill. Miss Earlene has been a housewife her whole life."

"They might be good stewards."

"My gut says there's something going on. And so did Dandy's. Did you know that last year Curt Walker went to Ole Magnolia on a full athletic ride? Did you know he went to Southern High for his freshman and sophomore years, and when he transferred to Courage High his junior year, he rolled up in a brand-new Silverado?"

"And?"

"His dad works for a manufacturing plant and his mother works part-time at the dry cleaner. Neither of their vehicles are anything to write home about." It was there in Dandy's notes with the distinct question: *Are incentives being given in order to come play at Courage High and even Ole Magnolia?* "Jared was seen with a lot of cash and front-row tickets to Aerosmith. Those were super-hard to score."

"But Jared already lived in the Courage High school district. Why offer him a monetary gift? He wasn't playing in any other district or planning to move."

"But he was planning on attending and playing football for Mississippi State until about two weeks before he died. I remember. And that's the same time frame he had a wad of green and those tickets. Plus, he was secretive about them. Even his sister, Amber, wasn't sure where they came from." Coincidence? Doubtful. "Someone gave him serious incentive to play for Ole Magnolia." Granted, Georgia couldn't prove it—yet. But it was enough to speculate over on her podcast and toss out her theory.

"It's not a bad theory. I assume you'll be moving forward?" Susan asked and collected her purse.

"I have to." For Dandy and Jared. If she was right and one of those men killed Jared, they deserved to answer for their crime.

Susan glanced outside. "I'd ask you to go get dinner next door, but I know you won't."

Dinner led to personal discussion, which led to emotional connection, which led to caring, which led to anxiety.

Nope, not pulling any triggers today.

"I gotta walk the dogs before the rain hits." The sky's last shades of pink and blue were sinking into darkness, and the forecast called for a soggy night.

"Fair enough." Susan pushed open the door. "Hey, you never answered my Would You Rather question."

Georgia grinned. "I'd rather die a violent death. I wouldn't want to be selfish. A killer not caught means the possibility of more needless victims and no justice."

Susan arched an eyebrow. "That's a commendable answer. On a serious note—you might be opening a can of worms when you don't have solid proof yet—I know. I know. You said it was all speculation, but if you nailed the truth, someone's gonna be furious. Having said that, when you do get hard facts, it'll be worth taking to Buck."

Georgia had every intention of informing the sheriff, who happened to also be Susan's big brother. "I will."

"You said it yourself. A killer not found is a killer roaming free, and on the off chance one of those names gets wind and recognizes it's them—or it hits too close to home about an illegal recruiting ring—you might be in trouble."

Georgia's chest tightened and her throat swelled, but she had a duty as an investigative reporter.

Susan winced at the wind picking up. "Just be careful. Maybe I'll grab dinner to go instead."

"Smart. I'm over the rain." Rain had been the wet theme to ominous news in her life—the day Jared was found dead, the evening she'd been informed that her parents had died in a car accident when she was only twelve, and the day she'd buried Grandma in the dreary, cold rain. Storms still sent a wave of panic into her chest, but she was learning to cope better.

"See you tomorrow."

Georgia collected her things and locked up. The dogs heeled to her Ford Fusion. They jumped in the back seat, and she drove the ten miles to the twenty-acre piece of property Grandma had willed her.

Up the gravel road on the hill sat her sanctuary. A house built to look like a cabin. A place she had trouble leaving at times for fear of all the danger everywhere else.

She unlocked the door and instead of the warm, enveloping freedom of safety, a chill slithered down her spine. Susan's words had dug under her skin and rattled her. Georgia's identity would come out, and everything she said would be out there. *What was the worst that could happen?*

She might get sued for slander. Defamation of character. She might have to go on record and retract something she said, and a lot of the town might ostracize her. *Can I live with that?* If it brought about justice for Jared, yes.

She relaxed as she quizzed herself with the coping questions Celeste had incorporated into her life. The fear of something bad happening was her biggest battle. The what-if question. It could potentially snowball until she was incapacitated in sobs on the bathroom floor over her child who died in a drowning accident. She didn't even have a child! Her imagination could quickly elevate to terrifying places.

So she had to ask: *What evidence do you have to support this thought? What is the worst that could happen?*

After she figured out the worst, the next question was: *Can I live with that?*

Once the negative thoughts were dealt with, they had to be replaced with something positive.

Philippians 4:8 had become another life verse. Instead of frightening or anxious thoughts, she focused on things that were good, lovely and worthy of praise. If it was noble or pure, she let it in to take root.

Anything else had to go.

Some days were bloody wars.

The good in investigating would be justice served. Lies hidden in darkness revealed. Closure for families. She could live with that.

But the nagging feeling something was wrong needled her.

"Okay, boys, let's go out before it's too dark for me to see." She opened the door, and they bounded out, barking at squirrels and at nothing. Typical.

Another set of chill bumps raised on her arms. She scanned her dimly lit living room and sniffed. What was that smell? Was she making it up, or was there a foreign scent in her home?

Her imagination was running wild, and she tried to shake the feeling that something wasn't right as she walked outside. She watched the dogs play for about ten minutes, then hollered for them to come inside. The full moon hung in the dark sky like something out of a werewolf movie. An owl hooted.

She rubbed her arms. "Come on, boys." Usually her blue merle, Doc, had perfect recall. Her tricolor was different story. "Let's go!"

The awareness that she was not alone didn't give her time to brace herself. A hulking man in black rushed her and knocked her to the cold hard ground. The dogs barked wildly as they rushed to her side, but they weren't guard dogs! They could get hurt!

The man's meaty hands wrapped around her throat and squeezed. "You had to go and stick your nose in where it didn't belong with that stupid podcast," he growled.

She couldn't catch a single breath. Couldn't think straight.

God, help me!

"Where. Is. It?"

"Where is…what?" she squeaked.

"Don't play dumb now. I want the information you have."

Dandy's notes! Giving them up wouldn't save her.

"I don't have it." She couldn't even manage a garbled cry.

"Liar. I'm gonna shut your mouth for good and I'll find it myself. Put an end to this and you."

She clawed at his hands, but he wore gloves. She thrashed like a fish out of water, but to no avail as spots dotted her vision.

The world grew dim as her oxygen dropped, weakening her fight.

Georgia was going to die.

Not without a fight.

Georgia kneed him in the groin. His groan roared and his grip loosened. Sucking in precious air and taking her shot, she scrambled out from under him and bolted. Screaming bloody murder, she hightailed it away from him, but out here…who would hear her? Help her?

God, make a way to help me!

Georgia headed for the house, but he cut her off. She

zigzagged and turned toward her half-mile drive that led
to the main road. Her lungs burned like red-hot lava, but
adrenaline kept her legs pumping.

Behind her, gravel crunched as he gained on her.

Colt turned on the long gravel road that led to Georgia's house. Lights glowed. She appeared to be home.

His stomach knotted as he approached. After all these
years, would it be awkward?

His headlights shone on a figure. Running. Wait. A
woman. He hurriedly turned down the podcast. Screaming.

"Help me! Help!"

Georgia! Colt sprinted into action and bolted from
his truck, racing toward her. Not far behind was another
figure. Taller. Bulkier.

She plowed into Colt, nearly knocking him down.
"Help me, please!"

Behind her, the man veered right, heading for the
woods. "Go get in my truck and lock the doors!" He
didn't give her a chance to respond. He chased the figure toward the tree line.

"Freeze! Police!" Colt bellowed and entered the
woods, but it was pitch-black and he had no light. He
kicked a fallen branch, irritated the man had gotten away.
He should have brought a light, a cell phone, something.

He turned around and jogged back to his vehicle.
Georgia had listened to him and was inside the truck
with a couple of furry dogs.

"You're safe now," he said as he approached, hoping
to put her at ease.

She stepped out into the darkness. Time had filled her

out and shortened her blond hair to her collarbone. "I've been thanking God. I'm sure He must have sent you."

He finally approached, and the interior light of the truck gave him access to better see her features. Dainty nose. Full lips.

"Well, you know what the Bible says about all things being possible."

She blinked as if trying to focus, then recognition hit, and she collapsed against him, wrapping her long arms around his back. "Colt? Oh, Colt. I'm so glad you're here."

Yep, it was awkward. For him. But he returned the embrace, feeling the softness of her body and the fearful shaking.

"Why are you here?" She drew back and frowned. "I mean, yay and all but…" Her knees buckled, and he caught her, moved a hair from her eyes.

"Didn't you already answer that?" He smirked. Humor was way easier than any other emotion that accompanied seeing, touching or hearing her.

"I did?" She seemed confused. "Oh." She laughed at her earlier remark, but it was fear-laced and wobbly. "Right. Well, I definitely prayed for help."

God had a sense of humor sending Colt, but right now Georgia was safe and alive, so he was okay being used in any way God saw fit. "Get in. Let's get on up to the house."

Once he parked next to her car and opened the door, the dogs bounded up the porch. "Can you tell me what happened?" he asked as he helped her into the spacious living area that opened into the kitchen. A stone fireplace nestled between two windows, and open wood beams lined the ceiling. Hardwood floors were dotted with colorful rugs. Yes, this was most definitely Georgia. Colorful, cozy and down-home. All the things he'd loved about her in the past when he'd felt gray, cold and out of place.

He guided her to the brown leather sofa and draped a multicolored quilt on her lap. Her hands shook, and she placed her head over her knees and breathed.

"Georgia?"

"Need…a minute." She continued even breathing, then deliberately raised her head. "I almost died, Colt."

What if he had turned around? Georgia would be dead. Now he was the one who needed some deep breathing. "Tell me what happened. Take your time."

She explained how she'd been attacked because she'd stuck her nose where it didn't belong.

Same reason he was here. But how did the attacker know Georgia was the podcaster? "Who all knows you're Christi Cold?"

"Just Susan Towers at the moment. Remember her?"

"Volleyball captain. She missed a serve and nailed me in the head during a game. Pretty sure on purpose. You and I were fighting and she did a good job holding grudges for you." He chuckled and rubbed his head as if it still hurt.

"It *was* on purpose, but I'm sure she's over it now."

"Let's hope so. Anyone else? Could she have told someone?"

"Nah. How did you know it was me?"

"I didn't." He explained who he worked for and what his analyst did to link Georgia's IP address to her physical address. It would take some computer hacking skills to do it. Would anyone who may have killed Jared fifteen years ago have those skills or know someone who did?

"Oh. Well, guess you've unmasked me."

"Yes, and it appears you've been a meddling menace." He smirked as the *Scooby-Doo* reference came naturally.

"Thanks, Fred."

He'd forgotten to miss this banter. "No problem."

"How long have you worked for the Mississippi Bureau of Investigation over in Batesville?"

"About four years. Was in Jackson before that." An awkward silence ballooned in the air. He turned direction. "Are you sure you couldn't identify your attacker? Even his voice?"

Georgia closed her eyes and after a few moments responded. "No. It happened so fast and it was pitch-black out. He wore black. He was as big as you. As for the voice, it was low and growly. Things happened so fast, if I heard it again I don't know if I'd recognize it."

Six foot one wasn't exactly unusually tall. That could be the build of a lot of men.

"Sorry I can't be of more help." She rubbed her neck, her fingers massaging over the small red splotches the attacker's fingers had left behind. Colt's blood burned hot.

"You raised valid points and insightful conjecture in your podcast, which we can discuss further, but right now we need to call the sheriff and reopen Jared's case now that we have a path to track down." Colt might not be able to finish up the investigation if it stretched past six weeks, but the investigators in his unit and whoever they hired for unit chief to replace him would be more than capable of seeing it through.

Georgia slicked her hair back, but it immediately fell into her eyes. "I'm going to make some tea. Do you want a cup?"

"No, thanks, but I can make it for you." She ran her

hands up and down her thighs, and her breathing was uneven. She might be talking a levelheaded game, but she was rattled. "I can talk to the sheriff and make tea at the same time. I call it multitasking."

She graced him with a tight-lipped smile.

"Sit here and get your bearings." He headed for the kitchen. "Point me to the tea bags and I'm gold from there."

"Thanks, Colt. By the way, our sheriff is Susan's older brother, Buck."

Colt cocked his head. "Didn't he used to faint at the sight of blood?"

"Still does to my knowledge." She found herself snickering and pointed to the cabinet above the microwave. The tricolor pooch followed at his feet as he called Buck and worked on filling up a teakettle that had been sitting on the stove.

He hung up with Buck. "He'll be out for questioning."

"I figured."

Colt dropped a tea bag into the boiling water, and immediately hints of something flowery and spicy filled the kitchen. "I need to see the information you referenced in your podcast—the evidence the attacker wanted. I also need to know how you obtained it. No giving me confidential information garbage."

He brought her the cup, and she thanked him again then wrapped her hands around the steaming mug. "It's at the *Gazette*. In a locked drawer, and it's notes, really. Ideas. The beginning of an investigation and a possible two-part podcast."

His frustration released in a pent-up breath. "That's not how you put it last night."

"It's a podcast. I'm allowed to embellish, Colt." She sipped her tea.

"You embellished a killer right to your front door. Well done," he smarted off and picked up his cell phone. "I have to call my unit. I don't suppose you'll allow me get you out of town while we investigate."

She avoided eye contact. "Negative."

He huffed and made the calls, then pocketed his phone. "Now isn't the time to be stubborn. You're not being weak by getting out of dodge to a safe house or somewhere more public. You're a target out here."

Georgia pinched the bridge of her nose. "It's not about being stubborn. Well, part of it might be. I owe it to Dandy."

"Why do you owe it to Dandy? Is she your informant?"

"No. She died four months ago. I found her notes." He listened as she explained how Dandy died and what was in the notes and where Georgia wanted to take the investigation. She was passionate, and he commended her for wanting to finish a deceased colleague's work. It was noble and there was merit to it. "She would have done it for me, Colton. I know it."

Colt would rather get her out of town until everything blew over, but she wasn't going to let him and he wasn't sure they had the budget to keep her up in a safe house if this thing dragged on too long. And it was possible. "Fine. But first thing in the morning, I want to see those notes, and we gotta figure out how to keep you safe 24/7. One of those names you tossed out may have been your attacker."

She dipped her chin in a grateful nod. "I'm sorry to be such a burden."

Georgia had nearly died tonight. They might not be a couple in love anymore, but that didn't mean he wouldn't always care about her and want the best for her. She'd been his first and only love. Fond memories tempered his frustration at not being able to get her somewhere safer. "Don't worry. It's my job."

And whatever it cost, he'd make sure he kept her safe.

TWO

Georgia awoke dazed and groggy, as if her attack and the reports taken by the sheriff had all been part of a terrible dream.

But it had happened. Colt's team would arrive later today, and they'd begin their investigation.

Now she smelled coffee and bacon.

Where were the dogs? She swung her legs over the bed and rubbed her eyes, then padded to her bathroom, washed her face, brushed her teeth and combed her hair. She moseyed into the living room, still wearing the sweatpants and sweatshirt she'd fallen asleep in.

Colt loomed over sizzling and popping bacon. Wyatt and Doc lay at his feet with hopes for a meaty morsel. Colt raised the spatula and a guilty grin. "Hope you don't mind me snooping through your kitchen drawers and making breakfast. I didn't know how long you'd sleep, and I thought you might wake hungry."

Mind? Her greatest daydream was a full-time chef who also did the shopping and cleaning. Her stomach rumbled, and the dark-roasted scent drew her farther on to the full coffeepot. No, she did not mind. She smirked and pointed at him. "And this had nothing to do with the fact *you* might be hungry? Not a single selfish motive at play?" she teased and poured a cup of strong, rich brew. Exactly what she needed.

"Okay, so there might have been an underlying motive, like my own stomach gnawin' on my backbone, but it's so minuscule it can't even be counted. Because really, it is about you."

She raised an eyebrow at his poor attempt at innocence.

"I let the dogs out earlier, but I haven't fed them. I found the food bin, but I wasn't sure how much to give them."

She left her coffee on the counter and fed the boys while Colt plated their breakfast and brought it to the table. She stole a peek at him as he laid out the napkins and forks. His clothes were rumpled, and his pecan-colored hair was a little disheveled. He could pass for a Hemsworth brother, looking way too good and scruffy for nine o'clock on a Saturday morning.

"After breakfast, I'd like to run up to the paper and get Dandy's notes." Colt scraped a heap of eggs on his toast and folded it over, then took a bite.

"Sure. Paper is closed on Saturday, so it should be a quick in and out. The dogs can have their walk a little later." Georgia sipped orange juice and concentrated on not staring at Colt's facial features and physique. Girls had dogged his heels since junior high, but he'd never thought much of it. Instead, he stayed more confused by all the female attention rather than flattered. Georgia had always found his lack of vanity appealing, and then when she discovered it was based on insecurity, it drew a deep sadness and a need to try to fix him. Colt might have always looked good, but his home never was. He favored his daddy a lot, but he'd never want to hear that he looked like his father.

After breakfast and mostly catch-up conversation, they loaded the dogs in the back seat of Colt's truck. "How long is ole Charlie going to run that show?" Colt asked. "He was putting out the paper when I was a kid. Used to give us suckers when we rode our bikes to town."

"He's retiring at the end of the year, and yours truly is next in line to hand out sweets to cute little boys. That sounded better before it came out of my mouth."

Colt chuckled and turned on his blinker. "Georgia Maxwell. Editor in chief. Sounds well deserved."

"I have a whole binder of improvements. Making it more relevant to our culture but keeping that small-town feel." She'd had her hopes up before, though. The past three years Charlie had told her he was retiring and passing the paper on to her, then every year about late December he changed his mind.

"Looks like we're both moving up in the world. Actually made something of ourselves."

She'd always thought Colt was something. His accomplishments hadn't made him the person she'd fallen in love with. It was his kindness, his big heart and the way he liked all people regardless of who they were or where they came from. As for her, the only thing she'd made was a life that kept her safe, except now she'd been physically attacked. At least she still had her emotional cocoon in place.

Colt parked along the curb outside the office. Georgia loved downtown in the fall. Big pots of mums bookended wooden benches that dotted the sidewalks. Scents from boutiques, bakeries and shops filled the air with the seasonal flavors of pumpkin, apples and cinnamon.

The *Magnolia Gazette* sign squeaked in the breeze. She would love to have control of this place. The first thing to go would be the navy curtains that had been pulled across the lower half of the large windows. "I have a key," she said as she retrieved her key ring from her purse. The dogs poked their nosy heads from the truck windows and barked. "Oh, hush, you two. You aren't missing anything. In and out."

She unlocked the door, pushed it open and gasped.

Colt leaned inside and whistled low.

The office had been ransacked, and papers littered the floor. Desk drawers had been emptied. Bookshelves no longer held a single book. Georgia started to rush inside.

"Whoa, slow down. We don't know if someone is still here hiding. Let me clear it." Colt drew his weapon and entered the building. After clearing it, he waved his hand for her to enter. "Looks like he got in through the back door. Lock's been tampered with."

She rushed to her desk and knelt at the bottom drawer. She'd locked Dandy's notes inside, and based on the scratched metal, someone had tried to pick the lock or bash in the drawer, without success.

Georgia unlocked the drawer and held up the notebook. "They were looking for this. I've never been more grateful for this ancient metal box." Newer models weren't as sturdy. "But I have a feeling they aren't going to give up so easily."

Her workplace had been turned upside down.

Colt pursed his lips. "I'll call Buck. *Again.*"

"Charlie's gonna have a duck fit."

Dandy must have hit the nail squarely on the head for someone to bring this kind of trouble. Illegal recruiting must be happening on some level, and it was possible

Georgia had identified Jared's killer. Between secrets that people wanted to keep under wraps and Jared's murder, things were about to go from bad to worse. Worse being more attempts on Georgia's life.

Colt hung up. "Sheriff'll be out ASAP."

Georgia called Charlie with the news, and after warning her to be careful but thorough in her investigation, he said he'd call in the staff to help with cleanup. An hour later, she and Colt arrived back at Georgia's. She turned the boys loose. They'd been cooped up too long.

"How long have you had the dogs?" Colt asked.

"About a year. They bring me comfort, and they're great watchdogs. They let me know when the delivery guy drives up, if a stray dog is in the area or if there's, you know, a dangerous leaf blowing across the yard." They'd tried to warn her last night.

The sun was bright in the clear sky, and the array of gold, rust, orange and crimson leaves showered the treetops with such beauty it was almost like nothing bad could happen. Smoke drifted overhead, accompanied by the scent of burning leaves. She ought to be raking, too. Instead, she enjoyed the quiet, the company and the sounds of birds twittering in the branches.

Gunfire boomed and broke through nature's noises. Colt paused and firmly but gently grabbed her forearm.

"It's Sunny Wilkerson. He shoots targets on his huntin' land every weekend. It'll go all day today and after church tomorrow. I don't know how Grandma stood all that shooting."

Colt relaxed, and they eased into a leisurely pace as the dogs ran ahead.

"I'm sorry I didn't make it to your grandma's funeral. I couldn't get away. She was always good to me."

"It's okay." She'd never expected him to come, but she couldn't deny searching for him in the lines of people paying their respects. "I understand you're a busy man."

He shoved his hands in his pockets. "We have all of Mississippi and more cold cases to evaluate than you can fathom. I wish we could get to all of them, solve all of them, but we simply can't. We're only four people." He shrugged.

"I imagine you see some fascinating cases."

"I do. And I imagine you want to hear all about them, Christi *Cold*."

She laughed. "What? It's clever."

"Oh, okay," he noted with a heavy dose of sarcasm.

"Okay, maybe not. But it sufficed." Until now. Now everyone would find out.

As they hiked into the woods, the dogs explored, and he shared several interesting cases, without revealing identities, and how he and his team had closed them— or were unable to. Those were the ones he said kept him awake at night. His whispered tenor tone captured her attention and kept her engaged, like spreading honey on a hot biscuit or listening to lapping waves on the beach at sunrise. "You ever consider doing a podcast? You have the voice for it."

"No. But I admit, I enjoy yours. I suspected you might be someone in law enforcement. You have the gut instinct, Georgia. For real." He nudged her with his shoulder and smiled. "You missed your calling."

"I don't think so."

They walked in comfortable silence.

Conducting pretend investigations from the security of her own home was a far cry from jumping into the throes of danger daily, like Colt. His career path proved her decision—though excruciating as it was—to break things off with him before college had been the right thing to do. She couldn't imagine the levels of anxiety she would reach knowing each day could be his last day.

Football alone had sent her into vomiting fits on Friday nights before games during football season. Her nerves would start jittering on Sunday nights and gradually develop and increase from worry to stomachaches to shortness of breath and irritability until by game time she was in the bathroom unable to function over everything that could possibly go wrong for Colt.

Life was unpredictable. Her parents, Jared and Dandy were all proof of that. And if sudden disaster didn't strike, there was always disease waiting to claim a loved one—like Grandma.

What if Colt gets injured and snaps his neck or spinal cord? What if he ends up in a coma? Or killed?

Grandma called her a worrywart and reminded her it was only a game, but Georgia had seen *Remember the Titans*. The same tragic accident that took the QB in the movie could reach out and take Colt as well. Turned out he never had more than a sprained ankle, but the possibility that it could have become reality was still seared into Georgia's mind.

When he told her that he made the college team at Mississippi State, she came unglued and had a choice to make. Stay with him, go to State and be sick and unable to function, or end things for her own peace of mind, even if it stomped on her heart. Georgia had crushed them both. Colt hadn't understood, and he'd argued, but Georgia had done the best thing for each of them. She'd had no way to make him understand how she'd felt, because he'd been right—it made no sense to worry herself sick. But she had anyway. He hadn't deserved to be saddled with her disturbing thoughts, and she'd needed the mental health.

Now, she understood her issues as a teenager. She wasn't dramatic or simply a worrywart. She had been suffering from severe anxiety.

Now that he was a law enforcer, it upped the ante. Just because he worked on cases that had gone cold didn't mean killers went cold. She was a testament to that. There would be no emotional ties to Colt. Never again.

"So, what will you and your team do?" She glanced at her cell phone for the time. The rest of the MBI team should be arriving shortly.

"We'll go over the past investigation, see where the case stalled and pick up from there. Talk to old witnesses and suspects. Run new tests on trace evidence. We'll speak with the coach and athletic recruiters at Ole Magnolia if it leads there. If someone was illegally offering Jared a sweet deal to come play, we'll find it. Coach Joe Jackson has been at Ole Magnolia for twenty-five years."

"Yeah. Wins mean coaches keep their jobs, unless another university offers more money. Guess no one offered more money." She shrugged.

"We'll call the NCAA and see if an investigator ever looked into Ole Magnolia around that time frame. They'll likely put an investigator on it now with the new information."

The National Collegiate Athletic Association had many investigators who regulated athletics across college sports, determining if colleges participated in prohibited behavior. Celebrities had just recently gone to jail for paying large sums of money to have their children enrolled in some of the best Ivy League schools—some on athletic scholarships.

"How can I help?" There had to be something she could offer the investigation besides Dandy's notes.

"Since the sheriff's department can't supply any manpower on this case or protection detail, it's just us four. You can help by allowing one of us to be with you at all times."

"Even in the ladies' room?" Sarcasm came naturally and helped her to cope with the severity of the problem.

"I have two female agents, so yeah. Even there." He gave her a take-that expression, but humor danced in his eyes as clear as mountain water streams.

"Whatever. Fine. But I meant helping in the investigation."

"I can't deny you're good at speculation." He checked his watch. "Let's get back to the house. The team will be here any minute."

"Wyatt! Doc! Come! Let's go home and get a sweet potato." The dogs sprinted toward her, barking their approval of their favorite dehydrated treat.

As they emerged from the tree line, a crack sounded.

Tree bark splintered above Georgia's head.

"Get down!" Colt boomed and dived on top of her.

Colt calculated the risk of running back to the house, which was about a mile from here, or hauling it deeper into the woods. The sniper likely had a scope, which made them toast in open range. His only option was taking Georgia into the forest for cover.

"This way," he urged and pointed her into the woods, shielding her from behind. The dogs kept pace, aware something wasn't right. The blue merle whimpered and stuck close to Georgia. Colt used the widest trees as covering, but another bullet slammed into the trunk about four inches from Georgia's shoulder.

They were dealing with an experienced shooter. His heart pounded, but he kept a cool head as his training kicked into high gear. Nothing mattered more than Georgia's protection. He yanked her behind a massive oak tree.

"Do you know what's on the other side of the woods? A road, a clearing?" he asked.

"We're on Sunny Wilkerson's land. The woods will lead to his cabin on the hill."

Sunny was their best option. "Stay low." Crouching, he hovered over Georgia as he used the trees as shields while maneuvering them farther into the woods. Leaves crunched underfoot, twigs snapped and the dogs barked, which would easily give away their position.

Suddenly, Georgia froze. Sweat poured down her pasty-white cheeks. "I—I can't."

"Can't what?" Was she sick? What was happening?

Her breathing became shallow. "I'm—I'm having a panic attack."

A panic attack. Well, she was being targeted for murder. "It's not uncommon."

She shook her head, but her gasps for air became faster and shallower. She could pass out. That would be the almost worst-case scenario here.

"No. I suffer from anxiety with panic disorder. It's common to me."

Oh.

"And I'm also being shot at, so there's that, too. I can't breathe."

She hadn't lost her dry wit. The diagnosis was new.

The dogs' continued yapping resounded through the entire forest, and Georgia was about to pass out, and he was trying to keep them alive. *Lord, I need some help here.* "Okay, listen to my voice. Breathe in. Deeply."

She obeyed.

"Look in my eyes. Breathe." He tried to keep his voice calm and steady, but time wasn't on their side. Another crack of gunfire sounded, but nothing hit directly. The shooter was targeting them blindly, which meant they were far enough away to dodge him. But he must know they were choosing to push through the dense trees to the other side. The question now was could they beat him across to safety?

She continued gazing into his eyes and breathing. Nothing romantic about this. Her breath began to even out, but she wasn't literally out of the woods yet.

"We have to act now. Can you make it?" he asked.

"Yes."

"Good." He clasped her hand. "'Cause you don't really have a choice." He yanked her alongside him and they hauled it about two miles, jumping logs, weaving between trees and pushing through brush until they came to the edge of the clearing. Colt had worked up a sweat, and his heart rate was up. Georgia had braved it like a champ and kept up with him as she regulated her breathing. He thanked God for the help.

In the distance, Sunny Wilkerson's cabin beckoned them like a lighthouse guiding a ship to invulnerable shores.

He checked his cell phone. Finally, some reception. He called unit team member Rhett Wallace. He picked up on the first ring.

"We heard shots! What's going on, Chief?"

"They were meant for us. Everyone's okay, though. There's a property on the east side of the woods about two miles down. A Sunny Wilkerson. We're about to make a break for it. I'm gonna give you five minutes to head this guy off in case he's following us." It had been quiet for the past few minutes, but that didn't mean the shooter had given up.

"Okay. Be careful. We're leaving now." He hung up.

"Five minutes and then we make a run for it."

Georgia nodded. "I'm really sorry for bringing you into this."

She had no reason to apologize. "You should be thanking me. Not apologizing. You'd be dead right now if I hadn't gotten involved."

"Not the words you use to talk a panicking woman off the ledge of anxiety, Colton." She continued her deep breathing. The dogs remained at her heels, waiting for a command. Now they decided to be quiet.

In five, they bounded out of the forest into the clearing and straight for the SUV full of his team members awaiting them.

A hulking man in camouflage burst through his front door onto the porch, a rifle in hand. "What's going on here, Georgia?" He squinted and came closer. "Colt McCoy? Harlan's boy?"

"Yessir," he automatically replied as his father's name roiled his stomach. "It's me." He wrung out of the timid schoolboy days and retrieved his creds, showing them to Sunny. For being in his late fifties, the man was still built like the defensive lineman he'd been in high school and college. "You hear any gunshots?"

"Just my own." His scowl swept over Georgia and the team members in the SUV. "I asked what's going on."

The tricolor growled and barked at Sunny. Georgia quieted him.

"Someone tried to use us as targets for shooting practice. Sure you didn't hear any shots?" Even his team had heard them.

"If I said I didn't, then I didn't."

If he was shooting as well and had worn earmuffs, then it was possible. Slight, but possible. "This is the cold case unit with the Mississippi Bureau of Investigation. We're reopening Jared Toledo's case."

Sunny's scowl deepened. "Why would you do that?"

"New information came to light. You wouldn't know anything about Jared being approached by either an athletic recruiter or booster, like yourself, to make it worthwhile for him to play quarterback at Ole Magnolia, would you?"

"Boy, don't think for one second you can come onto my property and implicate me in wrongdoing. I love my alma mater, but I'm not a briber. Get on outta here."

Boy.

The word flew all over Colt. The way his father spoke to him, especially when he was drunk.

Boy, where do you think you've been? Boy, you ain't worth a lick. Boy, you're the reason your mama left. Boy. Boy. Boy.

He swallowed the bitterness rising on his tongue and replaced it with practiced cool composure as he pocketed his credentials. "Mr. Wilkerson, I think it's clear I am far from a boy. I'm here on official business, so you can address me as Investigator, Officer or even Colt. We'll go for now, but that doesn't mean I won't be back with more questions if necessary. And be extra cautious since you're hard of hearing. Someone's out in the woods with a rifle, and he's a pretty good shot."

"Well, if he was aiming for ya, then I'd decline to agree." He spun on his heel and slammed his door shut.

"Well, he's colorful," Rhett Wallace responded as he unfolded from the driver's seat. As big as Mr. Wilkerson and full of dry wit, Rhett was not only a skilled agent but a good friend. He'd be the clear choice in leading this team when Colt left the unit. Not because he was the only other man, but because he was a stickler for the rules, levelheaded and objective. Poppy was a hardnose and often tactless, and Mae tended to be stubbornly biased at times. "You two all right?" He held out his hand and introduced himself to Georgia.

"I think we're okay." Colt escorted a shaking Georgia to the SUV and opened the door for her and the pooches.

Inside, Mae Vogel met her with a friendly grin. Mae was often underestimated due to her girlish features and petite stature, but it worked to her advantage often, as she was fierce when necessary. "I'm Mae. Nice to meet you."

Georgia climbed inside while Colt approached the passenger side. Poppy Holliday ambled out and tossed him a look of indifference. Muscular and tall for a woman, with chin-length black hair, she exuded the words *back off*, and she meant it. "Guess it wouldn't matter if I'd have called shotgun, which I did," she remarked and hopped in beside Mae.

Colt took the ribbing and Poppy's former seat up front with Rhett.

"I contacted the district attorney after you gave us the information last night," Mae said, "and she's willing to prosecute the case if we find new evidence that leads to a viable suspect. And considering you've been the bull's-eye for the last twenty minutes or so, I'll venture to guess our suspect is alive and knows there's evidence out there to convict." She frowned and pulled a strand of blond hair that had been tucked into the seat belt strap. While her tone was sharp, her pitch sounded fairylike.

"Also," Poppy added, "I talked with the sheriff, and the full case file, investigative reports, photographs, forensics, autopsy reports and video/audio recordings of those interviewed are available to us now. They're at the station."

"Good. The quicker we get to work, the quicker we can catch this idiot." Georgia had experienced a pretty hefty panic attack back there. The faster he could help her stay safe, the better her situation. He glanced at her in the visor mirror. She stared out the window, absently rubbing her dog and lightly chewing on her bottom lip. He'd have to research anxiety and panic disorder. He'd had some brief training for the job. Victims, witnesses and even perpetrators needed to be talked down occasionally.

But he wanted to know more.

"For now, let's get the files from the station and work at Georgia's. It's been a big day, and I think that's the wisest decision." Georgia had been attacked twice now on her own property, but she might, oddly enough, still feel safer in her own space, where she had some semblance of control.

"We'll drop you guys and then go get the file boxes," Rhett said.

Inside Georgia's, she went straight to the kitchen and began making coffee. Yep. Doing what she could control. From the moment she stepped inside, she stopped the lip gnawing. But did she not realize that she had zero control? None of them did at the moment. The killer could strike at any second. He'd keep that to himself and let her continue doing what eased her anxiousness.

Colt sidled up next to her as she put a kettle on for tea, too. "I know this is a lot. You're well within your rights to be afraid and nervous, and I want to help you. Could you tell me more about your condition? Help me understand. Find a way to work around it."

"My condition. Right." She pursed her lips.

He inwardly cringed at his terrible choice of words. But it was a condition, wasn't it? "I don't mean to sound insensitive."

"I know." She turned the burner to high for the tea as the coffeepot gurgled and the room began to smell like strong caffeine. "But there is no working around it, Colt. I can't control it. I can only cope using the skills I've been given and heavy doses of prayer. It's about working with it and through it, not around it."

"How long have you suffered with this?"

She leaned on the counter. "Twelve is when I remember it beginning."

Her parents had been killed in a three-car accident on the interstate. She'd talked about them often but never about anxiety.

"Started out not wanting to get in a car or wanting people I love to get in one. But I was twelve, so what I wanted didn't happen. It escalated to other worries. Worry about the world in general. I hated when Grandma watched the news at night. I never slept well after hearing it."

He'd always thought her freak-outs over him were ridiculous. It had caused a few fights, especially about him playing football or going out with the guys. Hindsight was twenty-twenty. How was a seventeen-year-old boy supposed to know his girlfriend wasn't being unreasonable and uptight but dealing with some serious problems? "I'm really sorry for being so jerky about stuff." No wonder she dumped him. He'd been insensitive and told her she was always overreacting and to lighten up. He'd have cut himself loose, too.

"You didn't know. And back then I didn't, either. But now I do, and I know my triggers so I can avoid things that set it off for the most part—some things I have to fight through, like driving a car and going out in the world to shop or do my job, and I have daily medication that helps me."

"Good. That's good, Georgia."

He wasn't sure what her triggers were, but he'd try not to set one off. Though a killer coming after her would be anyone's trigger, and he wasn't sure how to stop that other than finding Jared's killer as quickly as possible.

"Well, even with a panic attack out there, you did real good, Georgia. You were brave and handled the situation as well as anyone could." He laid a hand on her shoulder to offer physical support. How else could he comfort her and make her feel sound?

The dogs barked and bolted for the front door. A delivery truck approached, and Colt cautiously moved to the door. Anyone was a suspect in his book. The young guy bounded out with two large boxes and dropped them on the porch and waved. He returned to his truck and left.

"Are deliveries normal?" he asked.

"Definitely. I order most everything online." Her cheeks flushed. "Convenience and all."

And it helped her avoid a trigger of being vulnerable out in the world, where she couldn't control the environment. He didn't bother calling her on it. It clearly embarrassed her enough.

"And it helps me. But my therapist—Celeste—says I need to keep going out. If it becomes too easy to stay inside, I could quickly slip into agoraphobia. So I get out. And I ask a few questions that help me control my thoughts. That's really where the fight is. My mind."

"Questions like?"

"Like 'What evidence do you have to support this thought?' and 'What is the worst that can happen?' when I'm afraid or panicky about a situation. Then after I come up with all the things that could happen, I ask, 'Can I live with that?' and about ninety-nine percent of the time, I can."

"Sounds easy enough. I ask the same question working a case. 'What evidence do I have to support this idea or theory?'"

Georgia laughed humorlessly. "It's not easy enough. It's the hardest thing I've ever done, and I fail often. I don't experience life like a lot of other people. And that can lead to severe melancholy and even jealousy and discontentment. It's a big fat snowball, but it's not crisp and clean. No, it's more like a hot and heavy ball of tar gathering up all the emotions and sticking them to me until I suffocate." She blinked and gave an apologetic and embarrassed smile. "Sorry. Sometimes it's so frustrating."

"Don't be sorry. I didn't mean to be flippant about it." Georgia seemed fine on the outside. He'd have never known what was rolling around suffocating her on the inside, and he couldn't imagine what it felt like.

Scared to offer any comforting words, since he'd fumbled so many of the others like a pigskin on the way to the end zone with ten seconds on the clock for the win, he remained quiet, letting the room fill with awkward silence.

Saved by the sound of tires on gravel—the team arrived from the station with the case files. Spreading out at the station would have been more convenient, but right now it wasn't about their convenience. Though being surrounded by an entire facility of officers would have made him feel protected, Georgia wanted to be here. Now. So that's what they'd do.

Georgia offered everyone beverages and made them welcome.

Rhett thanked her and poured a cup of coffee. "What do we know about the grump with the gun on the porch?"

"Sunny Wilkerson?" Colt asked.

"He's a die-hard Ole Magnolia fan and one of the boosters." Georgia added cream to her tea.

"I know I'm from Mississippi and all," Mae said, "and I had a brother who played football, but I avoided it at all costs so…define booster for me."

Poppy spoke up. "I don't know how you managed to grow up in the South and avoid football. Boosters are representatives of the institution's athletic interests. They support teams and athletics departments through donating time and financial resources, which help student athletes on and off the playing field. In professional terms."

"And in nonprofessional terms?" Mae asked.

"They're fanatics! And the sort of people to bribe families, high school coaches and student athletes to play ball for their institution. Especially if they themselves are sinking heavy donations into the athletic department. They feel it's their duty to get the best team players." Poppy blew her bangs from her eyes and pointed to Mae. "But some just buy season tickets and tailgate at games with beer and crawfish, so I may have walked the plank with the fanatic thing."

Rhett snorted. "May have? And it's 'gone overboard.'"

Poppy ignored him.

Mae frowned. "So, they're informal recruiters for the college athletic department or even for the high school athletic department?"

"No." Colt jumped in before Poppy went melodramatic again. "Only institutional staff members can recruit for colleges. The NCAA prohibits anyone other than paid staff writing, calling or directly meeting with a person to recruit for colleges. But it happens. Quietly. High school athletic teams are determined by school district zones in Mississippi. There is no recruiting. However, there are some exceptions, such as teachers can send their children to any school district of their choosing as a perk, and then you can request going to another school, but there have to be mitigating circumstances such as heavy involvement in sports or activities—usually for upperclassmen who have already contributed to the school."

Georgia put a carafe of coffee on the kitchen table. "I think a booster approached Jared with monetary benefits to play football for Ole Magnolia, and because of the fake addresses used by players at Courage High, it's highly possible that the boosters recruiting high school boys also are involved with Coach Flanigan and possibly the college coach, Joe Jackson."

Steep allegations, but they held water.

Georgia laid Dandy's notebook on the table and explained Dandy's notes and Georgia's theory. "This is what the attacker wanted besides shutting me up permanently. He came into my house Friday night before I arrived. I thought it felt funny and noticed a foreign smell. But ignored it. Then he went all offensive lineman on me. But he didn't get the ball."

Georgia may have hated Colt playing ball, but she'd always had a love for the game. They'd gone to all of the Mississippi State games and even talked about seeing an NFL game for their honeymoon someday. But marriage never came. She'd dumped him with a lame excuse.

I don't want to get married, and what's the point of dating if I don't want a husband?

He'd been confused, shocked. *Since when?*

Since now. I think it's best for us both to call it quits.

I don't get a say? He'd gone from confused to angry and ready to fight for them. But her eyes held steel, and it was a done deal.

Rejected.

Gone.

Like Mom.

Dad had called the play, and it had run out exactly as he'd said. And if he'd been right about that, then he was probably right about all the other things wrong with Colt. But he'd been fighting those words, too. All his life. On some level, he did understand what Georgia fought. His thoughts weren't anxious, but they were damaging nonetheless.

He snapped from the past while Georgia continued to explain her thoughts.

"I'm not sure who Dandy interviewed—if anyone. She didn't note anyone's statements. I suspect she was gathering evidence quietly then planning to either pass it on to me, as the investigative reporter, or start the interview process herself. She never breathed a word to me prior to her passing."

"I can't imagine why." The Georgia he knew would have been on it like flies on a horse's rump in summer.

She returned his remark with a flat expression. "She died before she ever had the chance to uncover the full story."

Mae pushed her empty coffee cup to the side. "That raises a question then. Did she actually die in a legit carjacking gone wrong, or did someone stage it in order to shut her up?"

Colt and Georgia exchanged glances. It had crossed his mind in the news office, but he hadn't voiced it. One podcast using fake names and speculation sent a killer to Georgia's doorstep. Dandy's questions may have done the same. Someone was desperate to keep a secret and a possible murder quiet.

"Where did this carjacking take place?" Poppy asked.

Georgia told them what she knew and pulled up the story on her laptop. Dandy Martin had been stabbed multiple times in a carjacking that appeared to have gone wrong on a Saturday evening at the Wolfchase Mall in Memphis. MPD noted that there had been a string of car thefts in the parking lot and had asked women in particular to be careful. But no other victims had been murdered. Only Dandy. That alone was questionable.

Mae grabbed a pen and scribbled on her notepad. "I'll get in touch with Memphis PD and get the case information. If there were parking lot cameras, I want to see the footage. I'll find out the make of the knife used. That could be helpful."

"If they had decent footage, they'd have a photo of the killer. It would have been plastered on the local news already." Poppy stirred more creamer into her coffee. "Worth a shot, though."

"Jared Toledo's death may not tie to an illegal recruiting ring," Rhett offered. "All we have is circumstantial evidence. We need something concrete, but since the case is reopened, we should run all angles Georgia mentioned."

Colt agreed. "Jared didn't have many conflicts. He was a likable guy, but there is one hater. Chance Leeway."

"Who's Chance Leeway?" Mae asked.

"Played for our rival high school—Southern High. Both he and Jared were QBs." He tossed Mae a grin. "Quarterbacks. And he'd made some threats against Jared after the last game before Jared died."

Rhett noted that and thumbed through files. "I assume he was interviewed fifteen years ago. If so, it'll be in the case notes."

"Let's narrow down the possible suspects in an illegal recruiting ring Georgia noted in her podcast—the real names," Colt said.

"Obviously your Cougars coach," Poppy said. "I'd add the old assistant coach, Harry Benard, too."

Coach Duncan Flanigan and Harry had been a duo for a long time. Surely, one would know what the other was doing.

Georgia tapped her chin with her pointer finger. "Harry Benard is now the head coach for Southern High School."

"For real? He left the Cougars for the Tigers?"

"A year ago. There was a big falling-out between him and Coach Flanigan when he accepted the head coaching job. The whole town called Harry a traitor. Knowing all our Cougar plays. According to most folks—like Sunny

Wilkerson—Harry was taking our plans of attack right into the enemy lines."

Sunny Wilkerson was on the top of Colt's list as far as boosters went. He'd had time to shoot at them and make it back to his cabin before they did. He knew the lay of the land, too.

"Mercy, football is serious business." Mae whistled softly.

Colt watched as his team worked in harmony, making a game plan. Leaving in a few weeks would be bittersweet. "We'll start calling the people on Dandy's list. I want to know who owns 4214 Pine Road. Poppy, see if you can come up with the property owner. Should be public record. Also, I would love to know who penned that anonymous letter to Dandy."

"I can get you a list of people who attended the board meeting that night," Georgia said. "I imagine the letter came from a parent whose child wasn't granted permission to change districts. I'll have to go to the office for it, though. Dandy's files were backed up before they released her laptop to her mother."

If there was new evidence, they'd find it.

And Jared's killer would be found.

They only had to do it while keeping Georgia safe.

THREE

Sunday morning, Georgia woke and settled into her routine. She might not be able to control the case or the killer, but she could make her tea, read her Bible as the sun rose and pray. She needed the stability and security.

The attacks and the knowledge someone wanted her dead were paralyzing, but she'd been coping and she'd talked with her therapist yesterday for a solid hour and God multiple times a day. She wanted it all to go away. At least she had people protecting her. Who was protecting Colt? What if he got hurt? A tiny ball of worry pinched her gut.

Great, the tar ball was about to roll. Fighting it, she let the dogs out but refrained from going with them. It wasn't safe. "Hurry up, boys," she whispered.

The pups did their business and rushed inside, as if they knew it wasn't completely out of danger. Nowhere was. Not even her own home. Georgia didn't need to ask what proof she had to support that thought. It had been proven. The tar ball grew another quarter, and the pinch turned into a grip.

Replace the thoughts of no control with positive and

uplifting truth. God was in control. He knew who was after her, and He alone had the power to save.

Turn the worry into prayer.

Lord, keep me safe. Give me strength. I'm weak. I have no control. But You do. You keep me in perfect peace. You shelter me with Your wings and hide me. You are my rock. My shelter from the storm, and, Lord, if ever I'm in a storm, it's now. But I have to keep forging ahead. I have to be brave and courageous. I don't have to be afraid. You've said it in Your Word 365 times. Once for every day of the year. I will not fear. And if I do, it doesn't mean I have no faith.

"Good morning." A whisper drew her attention, and she opened her eyes. Investigator Mae Vogel stood before her. Not more than five feet tall, fresh faced, blue-eyed. She wore a pale blue athletic suit.

"Morning."

"I hope I'm not interfering with your routine." Her smile was apologetic. Georgia didn't have the heart to tell her she was. Georgia had invited the team to spend the night. The work had gone into the wee hours, and it was the least she could do.

"No. I made coffee, and the kettle is still hot if you prefer tea."

"Thanks. I love Sunday mornings, coffee and Jesus. I think I even have a mug that says that. Do you have a local church that you recommend? I like to attend when I can, even if we're traveling. Sometimes we all go together. Colt isn't awake and I forgot to ask him last night."

Colt had impressed her with his strong leadership and utmost respect for his team, and it was obvious they respected him. But that came naturally from anyone who spent more than five minutes with him. He was kind and commanding. Fair and friendly.

"He attended church with me, and I go to First Community over on Maple Street. It's past town square about a mile. But they have an online service. I'm going to watch that this morning." Her anxiousness would only serve as a distraction to anyone within five rows from her, and she'd end up leaving from being unable to sit calmly.

Mae poured her coffee and sipped it black. "Colt explained you suffer from anxiety with panic disorder." She laid a gentle, tiny hand on Georgia's upper arm. "We all understand, and this mess—these attacks—they can't be doing anything but ramping up the fear gauge."

Georgia appreciated her understanding and support. Another one of God's graces.

"Hey, good morning." Rhett Wallace entered the kitchen. Fully dressed and put together. He had warm brown eyes and thick dark hair with a little curl. He was the kind of guy a lost kid would single out for help.

"I'm going to church this morning. Colt said First Community was where he went. You going, Mae?"

"Yep. I have to get ready, though. Poppy is, too."

"Colt said he was, too." He eyed Georgia, and her face filled with heat.

"I'm sure I'll be fine by myself for—"

Rhett shook his head. "We're not risking it."

Everyone wanted to go to church, and someone was going to end up on babysitting duty. Humiliation washed over her, and the tar ball grew. Now it was punching her gut.

Why did she have to be this way? "I'm sure I'll be

fine. I'll keep away from windows and make sure the dogs go out before y'all leave."

"Before we leave for where?" Colt asked as he breezed into the room, dressed casually. Jeans and a Mississippi State hoodie.

"Church," Rhett said.

"Oh. I plan to read my Bible and watch online." He headed for the coffeepot. "Thanks, Georgia, for the coffee." As he strode by, she caught his fresh shower scent with a hint of masculine cologne. Couldn't be aftershave, as he hadn't shaved and sported a fair amount of stubble. Suited him well. In high school he never could grow a beard, and it continually irked him. But he wasn't a boy anymore. The awareness of how much of a man he was made its point every time he entered a room.

"Rhett said you were going to church." Guess he'd drawn the short stick. If only she could muster the moxie to go into the church and not freak out for an hour and a half.

"I said I *might* go." He shot Rhett a quick glare. "I haven't had much peace and quiet in the last couple of weeks. Sitting with my Bible and a cup of coffee sounds great, and I'm pretty sure God will speak to me through His word here or there."

Georgia scooched closer to him for privacy. "I know this is about babysitting me. I don't want to be your ball and chain, Colt."

He cocked his head, then that same spark of amusement she was familiar with lit in his blue eyes. "Well, I didn't ask you to marry me, Georgia Jane." His eyebrows twitched north. He was real proud of his witty comeback.

Georgia couldn't help but grin, though the pang of regret thudded against her rib cage. Marriage never would have worked between them. Her anxiety would cause problems and fights like in the past, and he would have finally gotten tired of it and left her in the end. She wouldn't have blamed him. "Yeah, well… I assure you, you wouldn't want that, either. I'm the weight everyone is dragging around, and I hate it."

"No one is dragging you around. You ain't but a buck ten. We're carrying you. Now, knock off the self-deprecation and tell me what you want for breakfast. We're imposing, and the least we can do is cook. We'll expense it, so don't start in with how we're dipping into our pockets to protect you. It's our job. Let us do it."

Not much rebuttal there. "Fine. I have waffle mix and bacon and—"

"You had me at waffle. Show me where everything is and I'll whip us up some." Colt clapped his hands and rubbed them together then looked at Rhett and Mae. "Y'all want waffles?"

"Does it snow in Colorado?" Mae asked.

"I want a waffle," Poppy exclaimed as she entered the living room.

"You always want to eat," Rhett remarked.

"Are you calling me fat?"

"I'm calling you habitually hungry." He frowned and helped himself to a cup of coffee.

After breakfast, the team left and Georgia helped Colt clean up the dishes, then they sat on the couch waiting for the Sunday service to stream.

"How do you think Coach Flanigan will react when you question him?" she asked.

Colt's lips turned down, and he cocked his head.

"I don't think he'll react well, either."

He adjusted the laptop and turned up the volume.

"Coach is a big fish in a little pond and has been for years. He's made his career on producing star athletes. His entire identity rests on that. His office is one big trophy case to himself. He won't like anyone questioning him regardless if he's involved or not."

Not to mention he'd won more state championships than any other coach in their division. "I know. He was steamed when I interviewed him for the school paper after Jared died." She hadn't suspected him, but she did hammer him on being lax with his players and allowing them privileges that could have gotten them in trouble.

"You mean when you went all Scooby and the gang. Pretty sure he made me run bleachers extra hard that day thanks to you reprimanding him for not putting cameras in the athletic training room and accusing him of allowing athletes to smoke dope and bring girls into the room at all hours of the day and night."

"I never thought that was smart, and it did happen. Nobody will convince me he didn't know what was going on under his own nose. He told me, 'Boys will be boys, Miss Thing. If you suspect Colt is cheating on you, ask him. Don't try to guilt me into installing cameras so you can feel better about your boyfriend.'"

Colt gaped. "No, he did not. You didn't think that, did you?"

"No. I trusted you completely, Colton. He shifted it on me to avoid focusing on his negligence and turning a blind eye."

"Well, he's going to be off-the-charts angry when he finds out you're taking another swing at him for something else. Unless he's the killer, and he'll simply shoot at you...again." Colt paused and held her gaze, then they both broke into laughter. Much-needed laughter.

"Or it's not him. Chance Leeway is a good lead," Georgia said. "What did he say in his statement from fifteen years ago? He was always a sore loser."

Colt shifted on the couch. "He lawyered up pretty fast—perks of being a criminal defense attorney's son. He claims to have been at the Dairy Freeze that Saturday night, and his two best friends backed him up."

"Any trace evidence you can retest?"

"Industrial carpet fibers that couldn't be placed at any one particular business. And Jared went all sorts of places and worked part-time for his stepdad, so they could have come from the dealership. But a print was found on his watch. No comparable match back then, but we're going to run it again and hope for a hit. Someone who wasn't in the system then might be now."

Georgia hoped so, too. They didn't have much to go on.

"Mae got the name of another major booster heavily involved in Courage High sports as well as Ole Magnolia. Terry Helms."

"He's one I was alluding to in the podcast." President of the First Hope Bank & Loan. He'd been a football king in his own right. Played for Ole Magnolia. Big donor to the college and all up in the Courage team's business.

"And a good friend of Sunny and Coach Flanigan."

"I wish someone would have thought of this fifteen years ago."

"No reason to. I'd like to swing by your office later and get the list of people and board members in attendance at that meeting Dandy covered for the paper."

"No problem." Three minutes until the service went live. "Did you know Chance is the assistant coach for the Tigers now?"

"I'm not surprised. He was a little king over at Southern High."

Georgia snorted. "You know his friends could have lied to alibi him out."

Colt nodded. "Maybe one of them is feeling particularly guilty for it. Over a decade is a long time to stew in lies. What is it the Bible says about sin?"

"Don't do it."

Colt laughed. "Yeah, but more specifically. Your sin will find you out. It's in the book of Numbers somewhere."

She hoped whoever had killed Jared—whoever committed that sin—would be found out.

Colt forgot how much he enjoyed being in a service with Georgia. Online or in person. The message had been extremely personal and relevant. Perfect love casts out all fear. People weren't meant to live in fear. Colt especially appreciated the pastor's explanation on what the difference was between healthy fear and the kind people weren't meant to live in.

Georgia had been silent during that portion. Colt used his phone to do a little research on anxiety, triggers and coping mechanisms. The team rolled in with pizzas for lunch, and they sat in the living room inhaling New York style loaded with pepperoni, ham and bacon.

Rhett grabbed a third slice. "Nothing on the casings or projectile we collected after y'all were shot at yesterday. I hope we can match them to the gun."

Mae snagged a slice of double pepperoni and ham. "I put a call in to the detective on Dandy's carjacking case. Hoping to hear something soon."

"I got us rooms at the Magnolia Motel," Poppy said

through a mouthful of pizza. "It's closest to here, so we don't have to impose or keep you up, Georgia."

Georgia paused midbite. "The Magnolia's pretty seedy. You're welcome to stay here."

Colt's research had revealed that sudden changes in routine or overcrowding could trigger anxiety and panic attacks. Besides, he didn't want to impose. Her world had already been rocked. "We'll be fine." He laid a gentle hand on her shoulder. "Our job isn't about comforting accommodations. We've worked in some seriously questionable places. One of us needs to stay, though—at night." He knew her best. She should feel the safest with him, but he hated to admit on a personal level he wanted to be the one to stay. He gave himself a good mental kick. He was here in a professional capacity only.

He had a life, and it was taking him to Atlanta.

Georgia had made it clear a long time ago that she wasn't up for marriage and, while at the time he thought it was a lame excuse to dump him, she wasn't married. By choice. He wasn't married, either, but that didn't mean he enjoyed being alone. Most nights he wasn't only alone—he was lonely.

"I understand." She excused herself to make more coffee. Colt motioned his team outside. The air had a nip, and the smell of wood smoke drifted into his nostrils.

"I didn't accept Georgia's offer because she was giving it out of southern politeness, but she's right about the Magnolia. It's the hourly rate kind of place, if you get my drift."

Rhett turned up his nose, and Poppy shivered.

"What do we do about protective detail?" Rhett asked and observed the property. He was an eagle eye, always on duty. "I assume you have a plan."

"I'll stay here at night," Colt said.

"That's convenient," Poppy said with a toothy grin. "Tell us about hourly rates then casually mention you don't have to crawl into motel sheets and risk bedbugs."

"Perks to being the unit chief," he teased. "We have history, and she may feel safer with me because of familiarity."

No one asked the question about how familiar they were with one another, and Colt appreciated the courtesy. He and Georgia were complicated. "The case is cold enough. I'd like to pop in and have a chat with Coach Duncan Flanigan."

"Well, let's get to it, then." Poppy saluted, just before a boom thundered then the sound of glass shattering sent them pulling weapons and ducking.

The dogs barked frantically.

Another living room window blew to smithereens. This guy was brazen to be shooting with a whole team of agents present, and that scared him almost as much as the bullets.

Colt raced inside while his team stayed low and fanned out. "Georgia! Call out and stay down!"

Another glass pane littered the floor, crunching under his feet.

"Georgia, call out!" Why wouldn't she answer? Using the couch for a shield, he surveyed every inch and spotted Georgia near the back door.

"Georgia!"

Bloody glass lay beside her unmoving body.

FOUR

"Georgia!" Colt's distressed voice reached Georgia's ears as if she were underwater. She grabbed at her stinging and throbbing shoulder.

"Colt?" What happened? One minute she'd been standing at the kitchen counter with a cup of coffee and the next, glass had rained down. After that, everything transpired in what felt like slo-mo. Hollering to get down, more glass flying and then an intense burn before she dropped to the floor. Where were her dogs? "The dogs…" she said weakly.

"Mae has them. They're okay."

Rhett dashed inside. "Everyone all right?"

Georgia tried to sit, but Colt kept his hand on her. "You've been hit, Georgia. I don't think it's bad, but you're surrounded by glass and I need you to be still. First responders are on the way."

Sirens sounded in the distance. Poppy swept into the living room, glass crunching beneath her feet. "Deputies are here, too. I see them down the drive. Looks like the shooter is gone. If he saw Georgia go down, he may think he dropped her dead."

Colt forcefully cleared his throat. Even Georgia heard the warning and reprimand in it.

Poppy cringed. "Sorry."

"Don't be," Georgia said. "You aren't saying anything I don't already know."

"Are you hurt anywhere else?" Colt asked.

"I don't think so."

First responders entered the house and made haste getting to her.

Commands, instructions and suggestions swirled together. In only a few seconds, she'd been lifted up, carried out to the ambulance and was being treated.

Georgia's brain was foggy, and spots teetered on the outskirts of her vision.

"She's hyperventilating," a female voice called then forced Georgia to focus on her and breathe deeply. Finally, it evened out and she was lucid.

"She doesn't need stitches," the female responder said. Georgia winced at the burn when the EMT cleaned her wounds. "You're a blessed woman to have few cuts. The bullet grazed your shoulder."

She was definitely blessed. Everyone had escaped with their lives and minimal damage. Colt had been out there in the open. He could have been injured or killed. Once again, her stomach knotted, and she worked to replace the thoughts with positive ones. Colt hadn't been hurt. He'd rescued her. He was trained.

The ball in her gut remained.

"Do you want to come to the hospital?" the EMT asked. "We have to ask, you know."

"No, thank you." If they could bandage her up and send her on her way, she'd much rather do that.

Only deputies remained as they searched the perimeter and talked with Colt and his team.

Her dogs bounded toward her, and Mae followed with a smile and steady pace.

Georgia loved on her fur babies. "You've had a bunch of scares, haven't you?" Shelties were prone to being skittish and anxious. The irony of her dog choice was not lost on her, but her babies were solid and appeared fine.

"I think we've all had a few scares," Mae said and patted Georgia's uninjured shoulder. "How you holding up for real?"

"God's grace is sufficient for me." The Scripture of her life, the one she banked on, lived by and repeated even if it felt like she was drowning in a pool of fear and anxiety. "But I kinda want to crawl in a hole and stay there. Also, I want to find out who this guy is and put him away for life. Not just for me, but for Jared." She could be brave. She could continue the fight.

Mae nodded knowingly. "That's the thing about God's grace. You don't realize what it will get you through until you're through it."

True. Georgia's imagination had always been grand, and her default was the glass-half-empty outlook. She'd never thought she'd survive something like being attacked and shot at—but it had happened, and she was alive on her feet. Terrified and worried about what would come next. Anxious over the uncertainty—but God's grace would also get her through tomorrow when tomorrow became today.

Colt rounded a corner with a quilt from her guest room and draped it around her. "Hey, champ. How do you feel?"

"I'm gonna take the dogs inside." Mae strode toward

the house and enticed the pups to follow with the promise of treats.

"I feel like I've been shot and bathed in glass. Crazy, huh?" She laughed, and it garnered her a smile. The lines around his deep-set blue eyes crinkled.

"Yeah. I mean, why on earth would you feel like that?" he teased and touched her cheek. "You scared me, woman. Scared me real good."

"Sorry. If it makes you feel better, I was scared, too." Still was. "More than ever I know we're onto something. That Dandy was onto something."

"I agree," he said and carefully put his arm around her. "Rhett and Poppy are inside cleaning up the glass. I'll call and see about getting someone out here to repair the windows. But we may have to board them if we can't get anyone with the right measurements in stock. I know you don't go out much—that the idea can set off anxiety—but consider moving to the motel with us. You can bunk with Mae and Poppy."

Enclosed. One way in. One way out. The idea pushed her to the edge of a meltdown. "I don't think I can. I know it feels like I'm being difficult, but I'm not." She hoped he could understand, but his lips turned down. He was clearly displeased at her answer. Once again she was disappointing him and being a burden.

"I'll make that phone call. Herb Jones Glass still in business?" Herb had replaced Colt's car window when he'd accidentally shot it out with a BB gun. His dad had lit into him—and probably worse—when he got home.

"Yeah. His son, Herb Jr., runs it now, though."

"I'll get his number, see if he can do me a solid on a Sunday. No windows mean extra vulnerability and easier access to you. All he has to do is come back and keep shooting." He cringed. "Sorry. I don't intend to scare you—well, I guess I do, Georgia. You're scared to leave but you need to be more scared to stay." He sighed. "Come on, you can't be out here."

Georgia followed him inside, the wind blowing through the quilt, leaving her chilled. Or maybe it was the hollowness she felt as Colt's words. She *was* afraid to stay. She knew the risk of remaining home. But he didn't understand. And it wasn't something that could easily be explained, especially to someone who had no idea what it felt like to suffer from this.

Mae approached her with a cup of steaming tea, the scent of peppermint reaching her before the cup. "Hey, thought you might need something to settle your stomach." She had a soft and easy way about her, but her gaze stayed alert and watchful. "I kenneled your pups for now. Keep them safe while they clean up the glass. Want some company?" She pointed to the two chairs near the front door but away from the windows.

She'd like new hardwiring. "Thank you. You've been kind, and I appreciate it."

Mae sipped coffee from a thermal cup. "Colt's worried about you. He feels like his hands are tied."

"I should go to the motel." But if she couldn't handle being there, the embarrassment would be too much.

"We got a nice fat break for the day," Poppy said as she entered the living room. "Projectile from the rifle yesterday match the bullets in the house. One shooter, or at least one gun. So that's good. Better than an army of killers trying to take you out."

Georgia opened her mouth, and Mae put a hand on her forearm. "Yes, Poppy. One killer is better than two. Just the comfort we need right now."

"Right." She gave them a thumbs-up and strode outside with a big box full of glass.

Georgia needed to get up and help with the cleanup, but no one would let her. Finally, they had everything straightened. Rhett held a broom, and Poppy stood in the middle of the living room with her hands on her hips, surveying the finished project.

Colt had a cell phone to his ear and a tape measure in his other hand. "Great, Junior. I owe you one, man. See you in an hour." He pocketed his phone. "Herb Jr. has the size of windows we need in his shop. He's going to get out here with a couple of guys and get it done. That gives me a slice of peace." The slight scowl let her know he held a measure of frustration, too. "You have too many windows in your bedroom, Georgia. Could you sleep in the upstairs bedroom? One window makes a harder target. I'd feel safer. We'll take three-hour watches, do perimeter sweeps. We actually have night goggles in our surveillance kit we keep in the SUV. It's not ideal. I'd like to get you out of town—hundreds of miles away. But this will have to do."

Georgia was overwhelmed. Tears stung the backs of her eyes. These people had come in and cleaned up her home, taken care of her dogs, made her tea—and she had no way to repay them. "I don't know what to say. Thank y'all so much for going above and beyond the call of duty."

"It's all good gravy," Poppy said and winked.

Rhett heaved an exaggerated sigh and slowly shook his head. "Just gravy, Poppy. It's all *gravy. Good* gravy is an exclamation. You basically said it's all good good. Like people saying, 'ramen noodles.' Ramen means noodle. Noodle noodle." He pinched the bridge of his nose, as if he might not be able to take one more word.

"Okay, so it's double good, which is better than one good. Either way." Her smile was smug, and she wiggled her eyebrows at Rhett. Utter disgust distorted his features, but Poppy didn't seem to be offended.

Georgia wanted to take a shower and hope it didn't hurt too bad, then burrow under her covers.

"I want to see Coach Flanigan," Colt said. "Bullets aren't keeping me from knocking on his door."

The fire in his eyes made it crystal clear he was on a mission and daylight wasn't going to be wasted.

Hopefully, the killer wouldn't come back tonight.

But he would come.

Coach Duncan Flanigan lived on Knob Hill in a large brick home surrounded by pastureland. Too bad Colt couldn't legally get access to Coach's financials. He'd like to see how he'd paid for this big home. If he was in cahoots with Ole Magnolia's coach, Joe Jackson, he could be receiving hefty kickbacks for sending him star athletes.

Colt pulled into the circular drive and glanced at Georgia. She'd asked to come since she'd interviewed him years ago. Colt wasn't sure at first if it was a smart idea—especially if the coach was the person attacking her—but then if he was, it might show in his facial responses. Of course, Colt couldn't arrest someone because of a physical response, but it would be helpful.

Besides, Georgia had excellent insight and reporter instincts. She would be valuable. And that had brought him to the next quick discussion.

"He's going to want to know why you, a reporter,

are here with a cold case agent. So how about instead of going in as a nosy journalist, you go in as a consultant to the case. If it wasn't for your keen deductions, this never would have opened up."

She seemed surprised then grinned. "I like it. I can add it to my résumé and then maybe Charlie will realize he can leave the paper in capable hands." She stared at the house and blew a long, heavy breath. "I admit I'm nervous. Not anxious, exactly. I could literally be walking into the lion's den."

"Well, pretend you're Daniel and trust the Lord will get you out without being ripped to pieces." He tugged on her hair in a playful gesture. "It'll be okay. Use those wits of yours and approach with caution."

"Excellent advice."

"Also, you realize by now that everyone is going to know you're Christi Cold."

She smirked, and his heart thundered. "I'm aware the cat is out of the bag. Would have been anyway, due to my own investigating. I can live with that."

"Okay, then. Follow my lead. You're a consultant, not a reporter sniffing out a story."

"Technically…" Her mischievous gleam made him chuckle.

"Technically, but for the sake of today…maybe reel it in, will you?"

"I'm not promising." She laughed. "I'm kidding. I'll be quieter than a church mouse."

They clambered from the vehicle, and Colt snorted. Georgia and quiet went together like sardines and peanut butter. "Lying is a sin, and what did we agree the Bible said about sin?"

"Don't do it?"

She was way too cute for her own good. He shook his head but remained amused. "Yeah. That."

A Silverado was parked near the door, and a lazy black Lab napped on the front porch. The dog roused as they approached and barked once as if doing the bare minimum of his canine duty, then went back to sleeping.

Colt looked into Georgia's eyes before ringing the doorbell. "I don't want Coach to be guilty, but I also don't want to go in biased. Pray for me?"

She rubbed his upper arm. "Already was."

A zing passed between them. "Let's do this, then." He rang the doorbell.

Coach was as much a legend today as in the past. He hesitated, then recognition lit his eyes and the pleasure at seeing Colt splashed across his face. "Well, look who it is! Colt McCoy. Number seventeen. Best defensive lineman in your class." His gaze moved to Georgia, and his smile faltered but didn't fade. "Hey, there, little lady. How are you? I heard from Deacon Tim at church that you'd been attacked and shot." He shook his head. "Glad you're still kicking. Come on in, y'all."

Georgia gave a small shrug. She couldn't tell if he wanted her dead, but he clearly held a little grudge thanks to her previous accusations against him. Georgia had always been feisty, and what Colt had chalked up to moody. Now, he realized there was Georgia the feisty go-getter, full of spunk, heart and ambition, who was hamstrung by her anxiety, which at times made her appear moody and withdrawn.

They stepped inside Coach's foyer. The house smelled of Sunday pot roast and potpourri.

"We're watching some recorded football."

Coach's wife, Earlene, sat on the couch with a glass of tea. "Can I get y'all anything?" she asked.

"No, ma'am. I'm sorry to intrude on your Sunday afternoon, and I hope we won't be here long. I'm on official business. So is Georgia—in a consultant's capacity. The MBI cold case unit has reopened Jared Toledo's case."

"Oh, really. On whose authority?" Coach asked. A stern expression only intensified his weathered face. The years had colored his dark hair silver, and his eyebrows had become more gnarled.

"Mine. I'm the unit chief. Georgia hosts a podcast called *Dead Talk*. Last Thursday, she revealed intimate information and her speculation about Jared's death and illegal athletic recruiting." He waited a beat, studied Coach's physical reaction.

"Do you have information?" He sat beside his wife. He was in his late fifties. Could he have the stamina to attack Georgia physically? He appeared physically fit and the right size, just older.

Georgia opened her mouth, but Colt jumped in first. "I can't reveal that and neither can she, but it's enough to reopen the case with a new line of investigation. That's why we're here."

"I see."

Georgia leaned forward. "Are you saying you're not illegally recruiting boys to play ball at Courage High and giving them a fake address to use so they can play in your district?"

"Excuse me?" the coach asked.

Georgia didn't slow down. "You haven't got some kind of deal worked out with a recruiter or the coach at Ole Magnolia to get those boys who play for you to also play for them? No monetary gifts to entice them? No kickbacks to you?"

So much for being quieter than a church mouse. Colt inhaled, exhaled and muttered, "Your pants are on fire, Georgia Jane."

She'd riled up Coach, and the last thing he'd want to do now was cooperate.

"You think I have to resort to that kind of nonsense? Has it ever crossed your mind, Miss Thing, that I happen to be that good of a coach and I mold and make boys into athletes worth having at colleges and in the NFL? I have had fourteen players go pro. You've always made false accusations, Georgia Maxwell. I told you that then, and I'm telling it to you now. No wonder someone wants you dead."

"That's out of line, Coach." Colt stepped in front of Georgia. Protective instinct as much as to shut her up.

Earlene scolded Coach, and that mellowed him out. "I'm sorry. But you came in asking if I was a criminal. One of my boys died. *My* boy. That's how I see each and every player on my team. Like a son. Not only did my star QB die, he was put in my athletic room. My boy. My place." His eyes held anguish, and he slumped. "I've beat myself over the head trying to come up with some information that might help, but I don't know any more now than I did then."

Colt believed him. Hopefully, it wasn't bias. Coach had been more of a father to him than his own. "Can I go over it anyway? One more time?"

He nodded.

"Were you at the school on that night in question?" Sometimes he stayed late in his office watching game tapes, going over the playbook.

Coach rubbed his clean-shaven chin. "I was. Not too late because of church the next morning. Jared came in around eight. Said he wanted to talk to me about something. But he got a call on his mobile phone, and when he hung up, he said never mind."

Colt hadn't owned his own cell phone, but Jared had possessed every new piece of technology that had been available. His father had left a hefty life insurance policy, and his stepfather owned his own used-car dealership. Colt had to have a part-time job and save for anything he might want, whether it was a Friday night burger and fries or college or even a new pair of jeans.

"Did he seem upset by the call? What was his reaction? Any idea who he was talking to?"

"No idea." He shook his head. "He seemed troubled, and maybe I should have pressed him. But I didn't. I was watching game tapes. I regret that."

Miss Earlene grasped Coach's hand.

"He said he was gonna work out an hour or so—after the call. I told him not to stay too late—church on Sunday. I stayed fifteen to twenty minutes longer and then left."

Jared came to see Coach and wanted to talk, but a phone call interrupted him and then he changed his mind. Either the call had something to do with what he wanted to talk to Coach about or after the call he lost his nerve and decided to go work out instead. Maybe to think over what had been on his mind. Colt had often done that, and even now he liked to work out and work through issues.

"I wish I'd have talked to him—that phone call…that might have been important, and I could have given him some advice. Kept him from going where he went. Kept him from…" He removed his hat and held his head in hands. "I can't ever get that guilt to go away."

"I understand. You couldn't have known."

Coach raked his hand through his thick silver hair.

"Can you explain why some of your players—two of them right now—are using a false address to play in your district?"

His brow furrowed, and he cocked his head. "First I heard of that. I don't keep up with addresses. I assume if they're in my school, it's all approved."

"Well, it appears several in the past and the two presently are using the address illegally."

"What's this mean for the rest of the season?"

Naturally, he'd be worried about that. Two excellent players were going to have to transfer to their rightful school. "What do you think it means?"

"I blame the parents."

"Rightly so." It might be possible a parent figured out they could use a false address and told another parent, who told another, but students needed proof of residence and a bill that confirmed it. So how on earth was that sliding by? Who was letting it slide by? Principal Wiggins? They'd have to have a chat with him. "They were being sneaky. I guess the school board will deal with the issue. But either way, the fake address racket is going to stop from here on out."

"And we'll be talking to parents and asking if they were prompted or assured they could use this address," Georgia added. "If you are behind it, we're gonna know. Sure you don't know about it?"

This woman.

"I think it's time for you to go." He stood, a vein in

his neck popping out. Georgia had a way of doing that to a man.

Colt thanked them for their time and stalked to his truck.

"So much for letting me take the lead," Colt muttered.

"What? I only asked what you were already thinking." She buckled up.

He started the engine. "I have a method. Angering him isn't it. I was going to build rapport. Good ole boy stuff. You nixed that in ten seconds flat, church mouse."

"I don't think he killed Jared. Do you?"

He was surprised at her conclusion, especially since Coach had acted aggressively toward her. "I don't know. I have to follow facts, not emotion. Time will tell."

"Did the sheriff's office pull the phone records? I'd like to know who Jared was talking to the night he died."

Pulling from the driveway, Colt grunted. "If they didn't pull the records, we will. If they did, they must not have thought it important. And it may not have been."

"What do you think he wanted to talk to the coach about?" she asked.

That was a million-dollar question. "Could be anything from the upcoming game to potentially feeling guilty over taking bribes to play ball at Ole Magnolia. We need to find hard evidence proving that theory. Right now, it's a good guess. Good guesses don't put away murderers or grant warrants." The best thing to do was work the case as if it recently happened. Take nothing at face value and hope for new information.

They pulled down Georgia's gravel road as Herb Jr. passed them on his way out, waving. "I hope they were able to get everything done," Colt murmured.

"Me too. I don't like to be used for human target practice."

"I don't like it, either."

Inside, the house was put together and in order.

"Everything's like new," Poppy said. "Rhett did the lion's share. He's a clean freak. We like that about him and that's about all." She winked in good fun at Georgia.

He surveyed the windows. Not a single smudge. "Where's Rhett and Mae?"

"Rhett is taking a perimeter walk. Mae is in the restroom." She gripped a red mug full of something that smelled flowery with a hint of spice. "What did Coach Flanigan have to say?"

Colt heaved a sigh and eased into the oversize chair across from the couch. When Rhett and Mae were back inside he gave them the play-by-play.

"I'd like to find the phone records. They weren't in the boxes of case files." Poppy stood as if that was the cue to let her leave.

"I can go with her," Rhett offered.

Colt nodded. "Let's meet back here in a couple of hours and we can order takeout. Call if you find them. I'd like to know who Jared talked to."

Poppy and Rhett left.

"I'll be out on the porch." Mae excused herself.

"Colt, I'm sorry for being such a bulldog with Coach. I guess if he is the attacker, I wanted him to know I'm not afraid of him or going to stop. But the truth is, I am afraid. Who wouldn't be?"

He sat next to her and the blue merle. "Like Pastor said. Some fear is healthy. But verbally charging him was reckless if he is the person who attacked you. So how about not giving me anxiety and quit going off half-cocked?"

She nodded. "Fair enough."

They sat in comfortable silence, thinking, until Colt's cell phone rang.

Poppy.

"Hey, whatcha got?"

"Phone records, but it's a bust. The call Duncan Flanigan referenced was a two-minute conversation with Jared's stepdad. He called to see if Jared was coming home or staying with a friend."

"What about the calls prior to that and after?"

"This gets more interesting. Chance Leeway called him at 9:06 p.m. Three minutes and forty-two seconds. But Chance lawyered up fast in the initial investigation. Not much to his statement."

"We'll see what round two offers up." If Chance was involved, Colt would find out.

FIVE

The sunshine had made a stellar appearance this morning, and Georgia had dressed in jeans and a fitted sweater. She couldn't let a killer keep her from doing her job, living her life. She was making progress, avoiding her biggest triggers successfully, though having Colt around brought up so many old memories and fond feelings. But she wouldn't let herself slip into those nostalgic moments, and she would not allow herself to feel new feelings for him.

Colt met her at the front door. "I had a feeling you'd be working today. Paper stops for nothing."

"No, and I have to make myself keep doing what I need to do. I've come too far to regress. Also, I do the crime of the week, so when you need to head over to the sheriff's office let me know and I'll go with you. Check the weekend crimes." She peeked outside and noticed a few boxes. She pointed to the delivery. "You want me to open the door or...?"

"Not even a little." Colt opened it, scanned the yard then brought the boxes inside. "Where do you want them?"

"It's the dogs' new beds and food from the local feed store. Kitchen table is fine." He set the boxes on the table.

Georgia inspected them. Noticed the tin and opened it. Sometimes Kate at the feed store sent home freshly baked dog treats. "Y'all got some goodies." She gave Wyatt and Doc two each and rubbed their heads.

"You hungry?" she asked.

"Don't cook unless you plan to for yourself." Colt sat at the table with his coffee. His hair was disheveled, and his scruff was turning more toward a beard. Didn't seem like he slept well.

"I always cook a little something. It's soothing to me."

Georgia whipped up pancakes and fried a few sausage patties, then brought everything to the table.

Indulging in extra syrup on her pancakes, Georgia closed her eyes and relished the deliciousness. When she opened them, Colt was examining the dogs, frowning.

"Hey, Georgia?"

"Yeah?"

"I think something's wrong with Doc...and Wyatt."

She whipped her attention to her puppers. They both were lethargic, and then Doc threw up. "What in the world?" She hurried to them. "Hey, babies, what's wrong?" She hadn't been letting them out to wander since the attacks. "You don't think they swallowed glass, do you?" she asked as her stomach knotted and a sweat broke out on her forehead. She couldn't lose her dogs. What if they had lacerations inside?

"I don't know. Let's get them to the vet, though." Colt kept a cool head and scooped up the larger sheltie while Georgia eased Wyatt into her arms.

"We see Dr. Reed over at Magnolia Animal Clinic." She could hardly breathe with every horrible scenario racing through her mind. She loved these dogs. She couldn't lose them. Why did she have to get so attached? They comforted her and the thought of their passing terrified her.

Colt hurried to the door, paused and swept the area. "Stay close to me," he said, and they rushed to his truck, where he loaded Doc and Wyatt in the back seat. Both dogs shook and whimpered. Dread broke out on her skin in chill bumps. "Climb in beside them, Georgia. They'll feel better having you near."

Crack!

Gunfire.

"Down!" Colt boomed, and Georgia ducked low with the dogs.

Colt dived to the ground, using the door as a shield.

Another bullet slammed into the vehicle and another. Georgia shrieked. They had to get out of here. Time wasn't on their side! Her pups whimpered, and Doc vomited. What was wrong with her poor doggies? They couldn't die and leave her! She prayed God would protect them all and spare her fur babies.

Colt returned fire into the woods. "Shots are coming from the southeast." He quickly called backup while keeping low. Using the driver's-side door as a shield, he slid into the driver's seat. Remaining hunched as he started the car, he stepped on the gas and they fishtailed in the gravel as they backed down the drive at top speed, but Colt never veered into the grass. A shot hit the windshield, spiderwebbing the passenger side.

"It was like he was lying in wait!" Georgia hollered over the shots, the gravel crunching and flying. A cold finger of fear scraped down her spine.

"He was. He used the dogs to lure you out."

Reality set in like rigor mortis in her lungs. "He poisoned my dogs! My babies!"

Colt slammed the truck into Drive and punched the gas, barreling down the highway.

"Are your deliveries routine?" he asked.

"Yes," Georgia whispered. Someone knew she had dogs and that she ordered supplies from the local feed store. Then the monster had the gall to intercept the boxes. But when? How? The tin. But how? "He's definitely local," she said.

"I agree," Colt added and flew through downtown, weaving and bobbing between cars to get them to the vet without delay. "I want to talk to the people at the feed store. Someone laced the tin of treats. Did they belong to the feed store?"

"I thought so. Kate often adds a little tin of homemade treats. But there wasn't a logo on them." Her neglect to pay attention might cost her dogs' lives. She wanted to kick herself.

"Someone who knows they often added treats waited for the delivery, then slipped a tin on top with hopes you'd do exactly what you did. Then he waited and ambushed us."

They passed the Magnolia Motel, the bowling alley, the small grocery beside it, and then around the corner the animal hospital came into view. Georgia bounded from the truck with Wyatt, and Colt grabbed Doc. Her head felt like someone had filled it with fuzz, and her lungs squeezed until she could barely catch her breath. She clung to the truth that God's grace was sufficient for her, but she still felt the raging fear. She hung on to the fact He was good and faithful and she could trust Him, but her insides continued to jackhammer. But truth was truth regardless of her emotion, which happened to be fear and worry at the moment.

The vet tech jumped to attention when they stormed into the clinic wearing fearful expressions. "My dogs have been poisoned."

"Right this way!" She ushered them into a room, and within seconds Dr. Reed entered, serious and moving with steady purpose. No time for chit chat.

Georgia explained the circumstances and symptoms. Dr. Reed wanted that tin of treats for testing. Colt called his team and had them on it. The techs ushered them outside into the empty waiting area.

Colt's strong arm pulled her close to his side. His warmth gave her some solace. She turned into his solid chest and cried. "I can't lose them." But that's what happened to people—and now pets—whom she loved. They died. They left her. Alone.

"I know," he murmured into her hair. "I know." He held her tighter. "I'm so sorry this is happening. I'll do everything in my power to see this guy is caught and does time."

She melted into his embrace, feeling safer than she had in a long time. His reassuring words slipped into the marrow of her bones. She inhaled his masculine scent and burrowed deeper, then caught herself. Oh, no. No, she couldn't allow any kind of feelings to wiggle their way into her heart. Feelings of safety would turn to dependence, and then that would snowball.

Then she'd care and end up where she started with him all those years ago.

She pulled away. "I know you will." She rubbed her arms where he'd once warmed them.

He searched her eyes with a puzzled brow. Her withdrawal had been abrupt, but it was in their best interest to keep things professional.

A few minutes later, Poppy and Rhett burst inside with the tin, and the lady at the desk hustled it into the examining room.

Now it was all a waiting game.

For her dogs' lives.

For hers.

Colt had finally coaxed Georgia to leave the vet clinic. Dr. Reed had informed them they'd caught the symptoms early. The dogs had been given crushed-up ibuprofen in the tin of treats. Kate at the feed store hadn't sent a tin this morning, which meant the killer had purchased the treats and laced them with the crushed pills. To lure her out for sure and maybe to even get rid of Wyatt and Doc so they couldn't alert her to his presence. There was no sneaking up on Georgia with the dogs.

Dr. Reed wanted to keep the dogs for a couple of days to monitor them and make sure kidney function was proper. They were safer there anyway. Georgia had agreed to leave and accompany Colt to the patch of land on Pine Road, but she'd been distant since she pulled from his embrace. He wasn't sure what he'd done wrong, but he felt the sting of rejection. He'd been there before with her. Withdrawing then pushing him from her life.

Better to rub out the sting and take it as a warning that getting close wasn't an option. There were many reasons. He could recount them all over and again. Time to draw the line between caring because it was his job and they were friends and caring because he wanted more than friendship and a professional relationship.

The latter wasn't possible. No point even entertaining the fleeting thought.

Now he pulled over on the shoulder of the road. The black mailbox with the numbers 4214 peeked out from the growth covering it.

"I'll be honest, Georgia. If Coach or one of the high school boosters are recruiting, the NCAA committee may only slap them with a fine. They could go right back to doing it again. I mean, Ole Magnolia might lose TV exposure if they're involved. Right now it's looking like there is some sneaky business going on with recruiting kids from other districts, but even so, the worst that may happen is a few penalties and public knowledge that they were cheating to win."

"That doesn't seem like enough to threaten my life or kill Dandy—if we find out it was staged to look like a carjacking."

Colt sighed. That's what had been bothering him all night as he tossed and turned. "No. Which means something else is going on. Penalties for infractions happen all the time in sports. That's why there's an entire committee devoted to investigating them. That's not enough to send someone after you—so it must tie to the murder of Jared. By poking around in the illegal recruiting ring, you've stumbled onto something far more sinister." His cell rang. "It's Mae." He answered and put her on speaker.

"Okay," Mae said. "I think we have some coercion goin' on. I spoke with Miss Thompson—Moore Thompson's mother. He's one of the boys who is using the Pine Road address. She refuses to talk to me without a lawyer present. So I tried Tyler Burgess's mom. Same story."

"They may be afraid of losing the scholarship to

Ole Magnolia. It's out there now. The boys will have to move unless the school keeps it under wraps, but Georgia knows, so expect it to come out in a news article." He grinned, but his joke didn't reach Georgia. She barely even smiled.

"Right, but I'm seeing a pattern," Mae said. "Single moms. Athletic boys. No dads in the picture. These mamas would be desperate to see their babies go to college, so fudging addresses would be tempting if an offer came through. And someone has gotten to them and given them the 'I want a lawyer' spiel. Is it worth pursuing? Poppy says they'll get a slap on the wrist and probably have to go to their rightful districts. I feel kinda bad for these mamas."

"If they're that good of a player, they'll get a scholarship without having to cheat. There are consequences to cheating and deceiving. It's not fair to boys who are doing things the right way. But I do feel bad."

"I agree, but Poppy says it's competitive out there. And if the coach or a booster is working with the coach at Ole Magnolia, then it's a guarantee only because of that under-the-table deal. They might not get it any other way."

Colt hated to see boys miss out on college, but this wasn't why he was in Magnolia. The NCAA could decide what to do about the boys. His job was to find out who had killed Jared, and if this infraction led to his killer—that's where his focus needed to be.

"We need to know who offered her the fake address. A lawyer is going to counsel them to cooperate. Either way, now that it's out, their sons aren't going to be allowed to play for Courage High. What school districts will they end up playing for?"

"They both live in the Southern High school district."

Harry Benard and Chance Leeway's school. Fighting Tigers.

Georgia leaned forward toward the phone. "I hate the situation they're in, but they made the choice to be dishonest. If we can get one of them to talk, we might be closer to finding Jared's killer."

"And your attacker," Colt said. "Mae, tell them to get a lawyer, because they're going to talk to us. Schedule an interview time. Have Rhett take lead. He's no-nonsense, and the lawyer and the mothers will recognize that. Have him crack hard, and when one of them breaks—do what you do."

"Be empathetic and sweet and get them to talk to me as a confidante."

"Whatever it takes within bounds to find a name. We have a killer to catch and no major leads."

"I'll have Poppy run interference with the lawyer."

Poppy was excellent at distraction and getting in the middle of something. He chuckled. "Get it done." He hung up, and they nosed through the mailbox—federal offense. Oh, well. Nothing there.

"Now what?" Georgia asked. "It's obvious no one is living on this land. I thought maybe someone put a camper out here, but it's not even cleared land."

"We're not far from Southern High. How about we swing by and talk to Harry Benard? Let's make sure Chance Leeway sees us, too. If he had any part in Jared's murder, seeing us at the school will rattle him. Feel like rattling some cages?"

"Do I feel like rattling cages? Me? I'm just a consultant." She feigned innocence, all wide blue eyes and pouty lips open in false shock. "I think it's high time someone else's cage gets rattled besides mine. I'm over it."

She seemed to be out of her funk—which he suspected was the anxiety. All he knew to do was pray for her. She wouldn't let him do anything else, and it wasn't his job. "Speaking of consulting, I'd like for you to sit in on our interviews."

Georgia expressed surprise then narrowed her eyes. "I feel like this consultant job is to keep me from nosing around alone."

Georgia had a way of getting into all sorts of hot water. He'd once had to save her from an upperclassman when she'd taken a photo of him at the movies with a girl—who wasn't his girlfriend—and posted it in the Whodunit column of the school paper. Whodunit—who cheated with Meg Frowlick? Cody Weinbeck. If Colt had ever known a guy to want to hit a girl, it was Cody when Tillie Maycott stormed into the lunch room and poured a Diet Coke over his head and shoved the school paper in his face.

"Two words," Colt said as he pulled back onto the highway. "Cody Weinbeck."

Georgia laughed. "Hey, I only did my job, and as my mama used to say—"

"'Time will lift the truth to the surface and it'll bob in the water of lies for all to see.' Yes, I'm well aware of that. You said it all the time. Guess you still do."

"Well, it's true, and Cody was a cheater and a liar. I just kinda helped his lies lift." She used her hands and pushed upward. "By the way, ole Cody is a deputy with the sheriff's office."

"Nice." He never liked that guy.

"He's still a cheater, too. Right in the middle of a divorce with Tillie."

"She married him? After he cheated on her?" Colt shook his head.

"Forgiveness is a thing." Georgia pointed at him and gave him a stern look. If she was talking about Colt forgiving his dad for being a drunk, a verbal boxing champion and a terrible dad, then forget it.

Colt's cell rang. Mae again. "What's up? We're heading to Southern High to talk to Harry Benard—"

"Yeah, well, he isn't there. I called to set up an interview, and the school said he went home sick this morning. He hasn't answered his cell or landline. That's why I'm calling. He might be a runner."

That's all Colt needed—to chase after a town skipper. "Give me his address. Georgia and I will stop in for a wellness check."

Mae snorted and gave him the address. "Jared's parents will be here in an hour. Don't be late." She hung up.

"Feel like checking Harry Benard for a fever?"

"I imagine if he's in eyeball deep, he's feeling some heat. Probably got the sweats."

"I know just the cure for that."

"Prison." She held out her fist, and he laughed and bumped it with his. Like old times. Partners. A pair. A couple. This was not keeping to professional lines.

He turned left as he came off the bypass. Colt still remembered all of Magnolia. Harry's home was at the end of a dead-end road on the left. His Mazda was in the drive. "At least he's here."

Colt led the way to the small porch and peeked in the living room window. The place was dark inside. No TV. Maybe he *was* sick.

"Colt," Georgia said in an antsy whisper. "Be careful."

Colt guided her back a step with his hand and drew his weapon. "Stay here. Better yet, go get in the truck and lock the doors. I'll gauge the situation and determine if you can come inside."

"What if someone is with him? What if they shoot you—kill you? I…" She fanned her face and inhaled deeply. That was her openly panicked face.

"I'm fine," he reassured her. "I have a gun. I'm trained. Please, Georgia. Go get in the truck. Go on, now." He gestured for her to return to the vehicle, then he knocked and tried the door. Unlocked. He opened it. "Harry, it's Colt McCoy. MBI. I'm coming in."

Colt wanted to shrug off the dark feeling that hovered as if something sinister had taken place. He cleared the living room and entered the kitchen.

Harry Benard was facedown in a bowl of cereal. Colt checked for a pulse, but the stab wound in his back made it evident he was deceased. He lifted his phone to call it in. A thud came from the back of the house. Quickly, he moved through the small hallway past a bathroom and two bedrooms. As he entered the master bedroom, a figure pushed a writing desk over, blocking Colt's path, then scrambled out the window.

"Freeze!" Colt hollered and maneuvered around the desk and clutter on the floor. By the time he climbed out the window, the man was bolting down along the side of the house.

Georgia shrieked, sending Colt into a panic of his own. He raced to the front of the house, and Georgia was a crumpled heap near the truck holding her arm. The guy ran through the woods at the dead end.

"I'm okay," Georgia called. "Go!"

He took her at her word and chased after the bulky man. Backup was on the way. After ten minutes of trying to find him, Colt realized the effort was futile, and he doubled back to Georgia.

Sheriff's deputies were on the scene along with his team.

"Did you see him?" Colt asked as he approached Georgia.

"It happened like lightning. I was getting in the truck, so I didn't see him. He shoved me into the side of it so hard—my shoulder—and then I fell and you were right behind him."

"*Just* getting in the truck?" He knelt and touched her shoulder.

She winced. "Well, I may have been debating a few moments about coming in for you. I was worried and freaking out."

"I'm not the one holding my shoulder." He rubbed his thumb across her cheek. It could have been so much worse. "You need it looked at?"

"No, it's gonna bruise like a peach, though. Was it Benard?"

"No. He's at his kitchen table. Dead."

SIX

At the station, Mae handed Colt an interview roster. "Jared's mom and stepdad are here." Colt hadn't seen Karen—Jared's mom—or Mr. Wilcox in forever. Chance Leeway's interview would follow.

"McCoy?"

Colt spun and Deputy Cody Weinbeck had his mile-wide grin going. He'd always been a ladies' man in high school, even when dating Tillie. He'd flirted with Georgia several times—until she wrote the article in the school paper about him. Colt had held Georgia's heart, and it had never made sense to Colt. How he managed to snag the prettiest girl in school was the greatest mystery he'd ever been tasked with and never solved. He'd been nothing but a loser with a drunk for a father and a mom who'd hightailed it out of town and didn't even think he'd been worth taking with her.

"Weinbeck," he said as he gave his hello in a chin nod. "How's life treating you?"

"Not bad." He glared at Georgia as if his cheating this time was her fault. Of course, Colt hadn't asked her if she published it in the *Magnolia Gazette*. Maybe she had. He bit back a chuckle.

"Cody," Georgia said with what appeared to be cool composure. "How's Tillie?"

Colt gripped her forearm with light pressure to let her know now was not the time to go picking new fights. Apparently, goading deputies and old classmates wasn't a trigger for her anxiety.

Cody ran his tongue across his teeth and flared his nostrils but said nothing. He stalked toward the alcove with the vending machine.

"Why?" Colt asked.

"I tried to help it, Colt. I really did." She pursed her lips and shrugged.

Mae looked puzzled but remained impassive.

Colt shook his head. "Come on. I'll show you to our case room."

Inside, they had access to a two-way mirror that allowed them to look right into the small interview room where Jared's mom and stepdad sat holding hands and looking optimistic. The team didn't have much uplifting information to offer, and Colt hated unearthing all that they'd worked to heal from and move past. But did one ever move past loss? Their loved ones would always linger, and the emptiness would always be felt. But a new, strange normal would eventually begin and nudge them into a land of living. That's how he'd grieved his mother leaving and never calling. Not even on a birthday. Colt was aware she'd moved to Phoenix and worked as an office manager for a heating and air company, but he knew nothing personal about her.

They entered the interview room and hugged in place of shaking hands. These people had been family to Colt and to Georgia. It was deeply personal.

Aging hadn't agreed with either of the Wilcoxes. Wrinkles and exhaustion backdropped the spark of hope in their eager expressions. He'd seen this exact face on nearly every family member of lost loved ones where no justice or answers had been found. No closure.

Gerald helped Karen back into her chair and eased his belly under the table as he situated himself in the seat with a groan. "Colt. We weren't sure what to think when we got the call from one of your unit members. Have you found something concrete to bring justice to our boy?" He held on to Karen's hand like a lifeline, and Karen sniffed. Georgia handed her a tissue from the box on the table.

Something concrete? No. Just a serious gut instinct that the killer had and still did reside in Magnolia. Someone Gerald could have sold a car to and Karen might have even given a haircut—could even be a regular at her salon.

"We've reopened the case based on new facts, which is promising. Now we can test the old evidence with new technology. The truth will present itself."

"New facts? Not concrete evidence?" Karen asked.

"It's enough to pursue."

"It better be, Colt. If you're gonna drag us through this again." Gerald's tone demanded they not be put through the wringer again. Karen closed her eyes, and Georgia grasped her free hand.

Colt asked all the same interview questions from fifteen years ago.

Karen was at home. Gerald had worked late at the dealership catching up on invoices and then came home, and he and Karen had made popcorn and watched a movie. They didn't know who could have killed their son. Jared didn't seem upset. No one that they were aware of had approached him about playing for Ole Magnolia, but Jared had changed his mind two weeks prior to his murder. Then a couple of days before his death, he'd confided in Karen he was going with Mississippi State as originally planned. They were surprised, but it was his choice.

Neither had new information to offer. Colt shared a little about the podcast and the attacks that followed and Georgia's theory about the illegal recruiting. Colt thanked them for coming and assured them he would not rest until he discovered who'd killed Jared, and Georgia echoed the same promise.

They saw themselves out, and Colt lifted his chin to motion Georgia toward the door. "Here comes trouble," he grumbled.

Chance Leeway strutted into the room. Time hadn't aged him. He carried the athletic swagger and had the physique to back it up. Not a fleck of gray in his blond hair. Clean shaven and irritated.

"McCoy," he said as if it were minutes before a game and he knew he was going to win.

Colt didn't ask Chance to use Colt's proper title. Didn't matter. He was in charge of this meeting whether Chance realized it or not. "Chance. Good to see you. Hate it's under these circumstances." He extended his hand for a shake. Chance shook it.

"What exactly are these circumstances? I need to be at the school, not here answering questions that I answered a billion years ago."

Colt clucked his tongue against his teeth. "Well, according to the reports from those billion years ago, you didn't say much at all due to a lawyer telling you to remain quiet. I don't see a lawyer now. You need one?"

"You tell me." His green eyes hardened.

"You're being questioned, not arrested, but I can read you your rights if you want me to." He invited Chance to take a seat with a sweep of his hand.

Chance scowled and plopped in the chair with a thud.

"Well, he's still a charmer," Colt murmured.

Georgia hid a smirk and sat beside Colt.

Could he be Georgia's attacker? Did he poison her dogs? He'd had time to kill Coach Benard, clean up and be here now. They'd spent over an hour with the Wilcoxes.

"Why are you here?" he asked Georgia.

"She's consulting on the case." He explained about the podcast and attacks.

Chance didn't seem too concerned for Georgia's plight. Didn't make him a killer. Just a tool.

"Tell me about that Saturday night Jared died. What did you do that evening? Do you remember? I know it's been a long time, man. I'm not expecting a sharp memory, but something. Jared might not have been your best bud, but he didn't deserve to die."

Chance nodded. "I respected his game. For sure. Look, truth is I was angry about the game the night before. Y'all won, but I thought the ref made some biased calls. I said some insulting slurs to Jared—to all y'all. I carried the grudge into Saturday night. After meeting up with some guys at the Dairy Freeze, I called Jared to apologize for the threats I'd made. That's why my dad secured an attorney for me, because that made me a suspect and he didn't think anyone would believe I was apologizing. You know he's also a criminal defense attorney."

Colt didn't believe it now. Chance wasn't known for saying sorry, and he wasn't even cordial about being here.

"I appreciate your cooperation. I'm well aware of teenage rage and spouting off hot air. How did Jared respond to your threats prior to your apology? What kind of threats, by the way?"

Chance snorted. "Typical butt-kicking if he crossed my path. I made it clear that I was the better player and everyone knew it. Face it—it was true."

It was true. Chance had had a better arm, but Jared was definitely scholarship material even without a deal under the table.

"Did you have a problem with the rumors that Jared was going to Ole Magnolia to play first-string QB and on a full ride for them, when you were going, too—with no ride—and were the better player?" Colt asked. "You'd have been playing his second string. I'd be fit to be tied if it were me. Because you're right, dude. You were the better player, and Jared knew it. Admitted it to me once."

Chance rubbed his chin and adjusted his ball cap that read Tigers. "I was miffed. Yeah. But not enough to kill him for a place on the team. Besides, he told me that night on the phone he was looking at going to Mississippi State instead. Probably wouldn't play much, but he wasn't feeling Ole Magnolia like he was before. I was shocked. He was gonna pick less playing time over all the fame and glory and the possibility of being drafted into the NFL? I told him he was an idiot."

Maybe Chance wasn't lying about the apology. He had just reiterated what Jared's parents had told them. Only Jared could have told him that. Colt leaned back and crossed an ankle over his other knee in a kicked-back, easygoing position. "Did he tell you that after or before you apologized?"

"After. Told me it wasn't necessary anyway. I was

gonna get all the playing time I wanted. Suited me. Why kill him if I was going to get what I wanted anyway? I had no motive."

Said like a true attorney's kid.

"How do you and Coach Benard get along?"

Chance grinned. "I like ol' Benard. He's old-school, but he listens to me, and quite frankly, he's been the mentor I never had. I've learned a lot about football from him. Why?"

"What do you know about illegal recruiting? Did he say if that went on at Courage High?"

Chance frowned. "It goes on. For sure. But not at Southern High. Benard is a straight arrow, and he wouldn't do that. Now, I can't say your boy Flanigan wouldn't, and I heard he has. Some guys I used to play with suddenly moved into the district to play for Flanigan. Rumors were it had been worth their while, and they did go on to play for Ole Magnolia, but I don't have proof. I guess ask Benard."

Chance legitimately appeared not to know Harry Benard was dead, and the fondness in his eyes when talking about him couldn't be missed. Didn't mean he wasn't responsible for Jared's death or Georgia's attacks, though. But then why kill Harry? "Was he at the school today?"

"He was first period, then he went home with sinus issues. I canceled his meetings for him." He leaned forward, his eyes wary. "Why? What's Harry done, McCoy?"

"I don't know. We went by there and he's dead."

Chance's face bleached, and his mouth dropped open. "Like a heart attack? 'Cause he's been popping a bunch of antacids, and I told him he ought to see a doctor."

"No, he was murdered, and that's all I can say, as it's an open investigation."

Chance sat stupefied, his mouth still hanging open.

"I'm sorry," Colt said. Georgia offered condolences as well.

"I can't believe it. Who would kill him?" He glared at Georgia. "Your stupid podcast. What did you say?"

"Let's leave Georgia out of this. I think it goes back to the night Jared died. But you had an alibi, right?" Did he?

"I was at the Dairy Freeze with Joey March and Ryan Sedgwick." But he didn't quite have the same confidence he'd swaggered in with.

"Got it in the files." He patted the manila folder. "They all said the exact same thing." And that was where the problem lay. No one said the exact same thing. They were lying to cover Chance's behind. But why?

What had he done that he needed them to cover for him?

And would they cover for him now?

Georgia thrummed her fingers on the interview table and rolled Chance Leeway's conversation around in her head. Colt paced from wall to wall while stroking his scruffy chin with his index finger and thumb.

She didn't like Chance for Harry Benard's murder. But she wasn't so sure he hadn't played a part in Jared's death and her attacks. Chance had accused her podcast of causing Harry's death, and if it had led to his murder, she would always feel guilty for that. She'd never meant harm to anyone, only justice.

Colt paused midway in the small interview room. "I'd like to take a crack at Joey March and Ryan Sedgwick. Their alibis are too tight."

"I thought so, too. They literally used the same words according the interview notes. Who does that?"

"Collaborating liars."

"Exactly." She tossed out her fist, and he crossed the few feet and bumped it. She'd forgotten about their bumps for agreement. One they also used as code to say *I love you* when people were around. Naturally, it was agreement only. But Colt caught her eye, and remembrance radiated regret and better times in those deep blues. Georgia looked away for fear of being swallowed and drowned by them. Instead, she replaced those thoughts with the case. Focusing on Jared and her own attacks was where her brain and her heart needed to idle.

The team entered the case room, folders and coffee in their hands. Their presence broke the connection bouncing between her and Colt.

"Did you get in touch with Moore Thompson's or Tyler Burgess's mom about getting lawyers and setting up a time to come and talk with us?" Colt asked. "And have you discovered who wrote the anonymous letter to Dandy?"

Poppy sipped her coffee and nodded. "The letter was written by a Shalondra Jamison. We talked to her two hours ago. She was angry over her daughter not being able to stick in the district for band, when athletes in the same grade were allowed special circumstances. She says everyone knows this goes on, but no one says anything because it makes the school look good, but she'd had enough."

Rhett jumped in. "As far as touching base with those students' parents, Miss Thompson is at work and can't take personal calls, and Miss Burgess isn't answering her cell phone. Her employer said she took personal time to go see her mother in Tupelo. Yeah, right."

She was probably getting out of dodge and hoping this would blow over. It wouldn't.

"Where does Miss Thompson work?" Colt asked.

"Wilson's Orchard."

He glanced at Georgia. "Feel like apple picking?"

"I was just thinking I could make y'all thank-you pies for putting your lives on the line for me." She winked.

"Don't joke about pie," Rhett said with a boyish grin. "Especially apple pie. It's my favorite."

The first time Rhett had lightened up. Nice to see. "I never joke about dessert."

"Then get to picking," he teased, and Poppy snickered.

"Y'all get some lunch and keep me posted." Colt led Georgia outside to the truck.

"So," she said while buckling up, "what do you do for fun in Batesville?"

He laughed as if she'd delivered a great joke. "Fun. Most of my time is spent working or traveling for work. And of late, packing for the move."

"That's right," she murmured. "Atlanta. Are you excited?" The thought of the dangerous and fast-moving traffic sent a nervous flutter in her stomach.

Colt twisted his lips to the side in thought. "I am. It's an honor to be asked, and I look forward to solving cases and proving they made the right call in hiring me. But I'll miss small towns and Mississippi. My church. My team. They're family to me, and you know I haven't had much experience in that arena."

Grandma and Grandpa as well as Jared's parents and even Coach had been more family to him than his own father.

"Have you spoken with your dad since you've been in town?"

He heaved a sigh. "No. He only calls if he's been on a bender and he's ranting about something that's my fault or that I can't fix. I imagine in person it'll be the same or worse. I have enough to deal with at the moment."

She hadn't had parents the majority of her growing up, but she remembered how much they'd loved her. Colt had never had that, and her heart ached for him. "I'm sorry. I rarely see him. Once at the farmer's market. He was buying corn. He was cordial, but it was small talk." Even if things couldn't be made right with his dad, Colt would feel better if he forgave him. She wouldn't press him, though. It wasn't her place.

"Subject change," he said. "Who do you like for Jared's murder?"

There were so many options. "I honestly don't know. Maybe we'll get a break and get an identified print off the watch, which will lead us to something concrete."

"Spoken like a true detective." His grin drew a gooey response in her belly.

Physical attraction. She could deal with that. Didn't mean there was an emotional connection. There couldn't be. Wouldn't be. "Armchair detective."

He chuckled. "Whatever you say, Sherlock. And I know we're making light—and I get the need to at times to help with the fear and anxiety, but I don't take your safety lightly, Georgia. I'll do whatever it takes to protect you."

Georgia paused, laying a hand on his forearm, the corded muscle doubling the response in her belly, or maybe it was the conviction in his words—a little of both, perhaps. "Thank you for saying that. I know I'm secure with you. My fear and anxiety—they don't have anything to do with your ability to keep me safe."

A sliver of relief slid into his eyes, and his shoulders relaxed. "I thought you might be triggered because you don't feel like I can protect you." His neck reddened.

Georgia's specific trigger, unfortunately, wasn't about her feelings of safety or not being safe. It *was* him. Or anyone she loved and cared for. Yeah, she was tempted to untie the bow to the romance box and jump all in, but she'd been there before—with Colt. It ended with fighting, her making herself sick with worry and Colt's frustration. Even now that he knew her fretting was more than that and tried to understand—she'd end up dragging him down and being a huge burden to him. He'd resent her and regret loving her.

"I feel the safest *with* you," she whispered. But her feelings didn't change the fear she felt concerning him or losing him if she let herself love him again.

He held her hand, caressed her skin with his thumb. "I don't want you to feel too afraid to experience life, Georgia. I don't want to be the cause of any of your fear."

She swallowed hard and fought back tears. To tell him in a roundabout way he was the cause would crush him. And she'd done enough hurting him.

"I guess we're both dealing with our insecurities." He let go of her hand.

"I guess so." While she ached for his touch, letting it grow cold was the smartest course.

As they headed for the orchard, she noticed his posture changed and he kept glancing in his rearview.

"Everything all right?"

"Yeah," he said.

Her stomach knotted, and she balled her hands in her lap.

Something was wrong.

SEVEN

The afternoon sun chased away the fall nip, but the chill that came from Colt's feeling of being watched hadn't let up. He'd been careful and hadn't seen a suspicious tail, but that meant nothing when his gut kept warning him. The last thing he wanted was for Georgia to worry. It was his job to protect her, help her feel secure and keep on alert.

If that meant apple picking, so be it. Even if he had to do it in a pair of khakis and a dress shirt. He'd suffer through, especially since he wasn't the cause of Georgia's anxiety.

Georgia had put that one fear of his to bed. When Jared had died, she'd retreated into herself, leaving Colt feeling cold, helpless and rejected. All he'd wanted was to be her safe place to fall, be her protector. After Jared died and it was ruled a homicide, Georgia had grown distant and become quiet. She didn't want to go out, didn't want Colt to go out or train in the athletic room. It had taken him weeks to convince her to go to the homecoming dance. He'd known he was losing her with no way to hold on.

Now, he realized it was the anxiety driving her away

from him. Another person in her life that she had cared about had died, adding on to the fears she carried about the world being unsafe. Here she was, though, braving the dangerous world to fight for truth and justice. She refused to cower and cave. But something nagged him—something she held back but he couldn't pinpoint.

He parked in a spot closest to the store entrance. For a Monday afternoon, the place was hopping. Several school buses were here on field trips, and moms were toting children across the grounds to the numerous children's activities, like pumpkin picking, hayrides, corn mazes and fun fall photo booths.

"Remember the year we came for the nighttime hayride and corn maze? That was so much fun," Georgia said, but her voice was shaky as they entered the barn-turned-store. The smells of apples, cinnamon and hay hit his senses and brought back the nostalgia of more innocent times.

"I definitely do." Mostly he remembered Georgia snuggling up against him, the feel of her warm breath on his neck as they huddled under a quilt while made-up monsters popped out and scared them during the ride. Protecting her—even from people in costumes—had filled him with confidence and a strong dose of male pride. In that moment, with her in his arms, he'd felt like a man and not a boy. He wasn't the good-for-nothing his father claimed. He wasn't weak or afraid. Colt could have conquered anything that night. After the hayride, they'd climbed into his first Ford truck and he'd most definitely kissed her like a man and not a boy. That was a night seared into his soul.

Was she thinking of those same moments, too? He stole a peek. Her cheeks were tinged pink, and she wore a sheepish grin that gave her thoughts away. What would kissing Georgia Jane Maxwell be like now that he *was* a man and she was all woman? His blood heated, and he wished for a glass of water to hydrate his parched throat. Instead, he cleared it and pointed to baskets of apples available for purchase. Apple butter. Pies. Jams. Pecans. Candied apples. "We could skip picking and go straight to buying. We're technically here to talk to Alma Thompson anyway."

"No. I mean, yeah, I'd much rather buy apples and text Alma Thompson instead of being here. But I need to push through. Keep taking one step then another. So let's pick apples. Be...be in the world."

Georgia had been through the wringer. Facing the world—the place she feared most—was amazing to him. She was a fighter, not taking the easy way out. He'd keep his eyes peeled and make sure no harm came to her.

The manager led them to the employee lounge, where Alma Thompson sat picking at a salad. With hair grayer than he expected for her forty-two years and eyes revealing even more layers of exhaustion, she laid down her fork.

He made introductions. She tensed and followed up with the need for her lawyer.

That didn't surprise him. "No problem. But if you're afraid of getting in trouble for accepting gifts and a proposal to see your boy go to college for free, don't be. You can't get in trouble for that."

Georgia sat down, straightened her purse that was hanging across her middle and scooted her chair closer to Miss Thompson. "My friend Jared played ball like your Moore. He had a family. A mom who doted on him and bragged about his athletic ability. She would love to know who stole him away before his time. Wouldn't you want to know if the tables were turned? By talking to us, you could help us find out."

Miss Thompson shed a tear. "I have to live in this county. Work here. I can't…I can't help you."

"But someone did approach you about using the Pine Road address so Moore could play at Courage High. Maybe even helped you out a little financially?" Colt asked.

She gave one almost invisible nod.

"How did you get away with the proof of residence?" Georgia asked.

She ran her hands through her hair. "I was told it would all be taken care of. Moore would be in a state championship district and molded into a player who would get a full ride, barring injury that would keep him from playing."

"Please give us a name. Please," Georgia begged. "One name and we'll leave."

She chewed her lip, clearly torn about doing the right thing. Finally she spoke. "It was Coach Benard. He came to my house two months before Moore's freshman year. He offered me four thousand dollars and a promise he could go to college for free, and six months of my mortgage was paid. He'll graduate next year, and he's going to Ole Magnolia. First in my family to ever go to college."

Harry Benard. He wouldn't be telling them anything. "Did he come to you in the last week or two about anything?"

"Yes. He stopped by Sunday night. Told me if anyone came calling to say I wanted a lawyer. I told him I couldn't pay for a lawyer, but he said not to worry. One would be provided for free. Then he gave me a card." She reached into her purse and handed Colt the business card.

Reggie Leeway.

Chance Leeway's dad. Well, that was interesting.

"Is my boy going to have to return to Southern High? Will he lose his free ride? That was the deal. He had to play for the Cougars—even when Coach Benard transferred. I asked…but the deal was the deal."

Again. Interesting.

"I don't know about college." Colt stood. "But my guess is he'll have to transfer back to Southern High. They have a good program. He still might be able to get an athletic scholarship." But not guaranteed. He refrained from sharing that Coach Benard had been killed. He sympathized with the single mom, and she had enough to deal with at the moment. They left her and strode through the store into a designated kid area full of games and rides.

"Coach Flanigan had to know. Why else couldn't Moore transfer with Benard?" Colt asked.

"Maybe the deal wasn't with Flanigan but Coach Jackson and Benard, or a booster and Benard. He might have known, though—or turned a blind eye. Flanigan was good at that."

"True." He surveyed their surroundings, an eerie feeling creeping into his chest. "And Reggie Leeway? Why would he be on retainer for an illegal recruiting ring that didn't even help out his own son?"

"I don't know. Maybe the money was worth it. His son didn't need a scholarship like those other boys." Georgia frowned. "Reggie Leeway might simply be an opportunist."

Or the plot was thickening. There was entirely too

much connection. Mae should know by now who that property belonged to on Pine Road. He whipped out his cell and called her. She answered on the third ring.

"Let me guess, you want to know who owns the property on Pine Road."

"Mind reader."

"It was purchased by a James Kreger, but here's the dealio. I can't find a legit James Kreger who owns the property. Nothing."

Colt relayed their conversation with Miss Thompson, then he hung up. "This thing gets deeper every second."

"I feel like we're already drowning in it." Georgia inhaled and closed her eyes. "I love fall, and all this is ruining it."

"I know," he murmured.

She opened her eyes and held his gaze. Man, she was beautiful. He searched her eyes, almost as blue as the Los Angeles Chargers' new jerseys. What thoughts was she holding behind them? Were they anywhere near on the level of his?

All he wanted to do was lean down and kiss her, taste those soft lips and melt into her, but that would be detrimental. Instead, he tousled the sloppy bun on her head. Strands of blond hair spilled out, and little pieces framed her face and brushed her neck. Way more appealing than she probably intended it to be. He could envision her in one of his flannels—all oversize with the sleeves rolled up and a pair of worn jeans that fit in all the perfect places, helping him rake leaves. He could imagine them falling into those piles of leaves... He shook out of the thought and mentally rapped himself upside the head.

She didn't want you. Didn't want anyone, and she

*clearly doesn't want anyone now or she'd be with some-
one, and it wouldn't be you.*

The tractor to take them to the apple-picking spot
rumbled to a stop, but they remained locked in on one
another, the air thickening between them and longing
nipping at their heels. It was all there in the connection.

Someone cleared their throat, forcing him to avert his
attention and let the moment go.

"It's a kid-friendly atmosphere, y'all." The redhead
snickered and recognition dawned.

"Daisy Miller?"

"It's March now. I married Joey March."

Joey March was one of Chance Leeway's alibis for
the night Jared died.

"Hey, Georgia," Daisy drawled as they scrambled into
the trailer and chose two hay bales near the tailgate.
Daisy, her two friends and their cluster of kids were
closer to the tractor.

Georgia exchanged pleasantries with their old class-
mate. Daisy hadn't dated Joey in high school—that
would have been social suicide, being from a rival team.

"I saw Chance earlier today. Joey and him still run
around?" Colt asked.

"Some. Joey stays busy at the lumberyard, but we
don't miss a game."

"Rootin' for Tigers or Cougars? Traitor," he joked.

"Well, Tigers, of course. Unless we play the Cougars, and then I secretly root for them. But don't go
tellin' anyone I said that." The ladies with her giggled,
and one of them reprimanded her youngest from hanging over the wagon.

"Go to my grave."

"Joey said you was looking into Jared's death. One

of your people called him about an interview, and he talked to Chance earlier today." She glanced at Georgia. "Rumor has it you're Christi Cold—lady doin' those cold case podcasts. Is it true the killer heard about what happened and tried to kill you?"

Georgia's body tensed, and she rubbed her lips together. "It's true."

Daisy pointed to Colt. "So you came to her rescue," she said with a sugary smile and innuendo in her eye.

"I'm here to do my job, Daisy. That's all." The last thing he needed was to leave Magnolia with rumors afloat about some nonexistent love affair between him and Georgia. Small towns talked. Didn't have to be true.

Georgia bristled.

Daisy smirked and wrangled one of her kiddos from climbing on the remaining hay bales. As they approached the orchard, Daisy leaned in, all teasing gone. "Chance would never have hurt Jared. He was mouthy and you know that. Don't let old rival feelings sway your good common sense, Colt." The wagon came to a stop, and she ushered her two kids into the orchard.

Was that what the town thought? That Colt was leading the investigation with hard feelings over facts and evidence? "I would never do that," he insisted and helped Georgia off the wagon. The driver handed out lightweight wooden buckets with handles for apple picking.

Georgia took two and handed one to Colt. "Daisy's always been a fan of the rumor mill. Don't let her get to you. No one with any sense believes you're using the case to settle an old football score." She reached up and lightly touched his cheek. "Let's pick apples and pretend we didn't see her. Or we could look at the insight she gave us."

"I like all the above aversions." And the way she touched him. But he could do without the way it shifted and moved him inside.

Georgia suddenly removed her hand and balled it by her side. "Daisy tipped us off by telling us that Chance immediately called Joey after the interview. Probably to remind him of his alibi and to talk about the case. Now, all of a sudden, they turn it on you and not them. You've come to throw around your professional weight and settle an old score. Innocent, sane people do not start rumors like that. Disgruntled people, or people with secrets, make up trash." She gave him a knowing look and plucked an apple.

"Georgia, you really did miss your calling." He picked an apple and bit into it. The fresh, sweet taste covered his tongue, and the day started to look up. "Let's ferret this secret out and put an end to rumors."

"McCoy, I like that idea."

And put an end to the attacks on her life. That went without saying.

Colt turned as the wind blew a chill across his neck. Or was it the sensation in his gut that warned him they weren't alone?

Georgia had filled a bucket's worth of apples. She'd be making pies, plural, along with every other apple recipe known to man, but what tasted the sweetest was the feeling of freedom in today. She strolled through the trees, smelling the fruity scent of apples and fall with Colt a foot away. In the last hour, he'd become distracted and received several phone calls, but when Georgia had asked him if he was ready to go back, he'd declined.

Guess he needed the fresh air and change of scenery as much as she did. Sometimes a new atmosphere gave a new perspective. For this moment, life felt safe and enjoyable.

Colt's presence beside her gave her a boost of confidence and a flutter in her belly—which didn't belong—but the flutter in itself felt good. She glanced up at him as he plucked an apple. Even his pleasing scent was more masculine than she remembered. About an hour ago, he'd almost kissed her. His eyes had revealed his intent.

And even knowing it would be disastrous, she would have let him.

It wasn't his rugged appeal or masculine physique. It wasn't the fact she'd been lonely for years and had resigned herself to it. It wasn't even the hyperawareness of a man she was attracted to bringing out some kind of hormone. No, these stupid, useless feelings had cropped up in the way Colt confidently and quietly led her to safe places, the way he shielded her from Chance's ugly words like he was a solid wall that had to be pierced before an attempt could be made on her, and it was in the strength he showed as a team leader, displaying wisdom to protect her and his people.

It wasn't that his smile was amazing but the way it reassured her that things would turn out for the good. These crazy feelings weren't born from his gorgeous blue eyes, but from the way they held tenderness and fierceness at once and his hopeful attitude and his thirst for justice. In a horrible situation where she ought to be cowering, he could make her laugh. And yes, she yearned for his touch, not because of the physical pull it brought but the ember of hope that maybe love was worth the worry and the risk.

She was taking it one day at a time. It might be worth the roller coaster of emotions.

"Georgia," Colt called.

She blinked out of the thoughts that had her easing from her fortress of solitude and opening up to the idea of falling in love—not with just anyone but with Colt.

"It's time to go. As much as I'd love to stay." Pain colored his voice, and she wondered if he meant this moment or when the case closed and he had to leave for Atlanta. Which brought on another heap of anxiety. If she opened up to the possibility of a relationship with him—if he even wanted one—then that would mean uprooting everything she loved and that was familiar to her, and giving up the editor in chief position, which she'd wanted for years, all to go somewhere unknown, unfamiliar and fast-paced.

She wanted to prolong their time. Their reality was threats and mayhem. "How about we walk back instead of taking the hayride?"

He paused and searched her eyes. "Yeah. Let's walk. I'm over bumpy rides."

Nothing was truer. Life had been a bumpy ride for them both. No way to control the dips, divots and ditches. Colt tried to control it by fighting the past with cold cases. She tried to control it by isolation. Did he feel the vacuum sucking up all the joy and surprises in life as much as she did?

Colt took her heavy basket of apples, and they strolled in silence to the barn entrance, where employees weighed their apples and Colt purchased them. Colt scoured the lot and kept Georgia close to him. "Ready?"

For reality? No. "I would like to visit my fur babies

later, if it's okay. To at least let them know I haven't abandoned them."

A flash of sorrow passed over Colt's face. Abandonment. His mother must have popped into his mind with that word. But Georgia was certain their last conversation before they broke up would echo in his ears. It was one of the last words he'd hurled at Georgia when she ended their relationship.

You're going to leave me? Abandon me? Did you ever love me at all?

And Georgia had lied.

I don't know.

It killed her even now to think about it, but she hadn't had the fight in her to keep him at bay, so she'd had to hurt him to heal and help him. At least, at the time, that's what she'd thought she was doing—helping and healing.

Now, she regretted what her teenage self had done. Lying never was the right thing in any circumstance. Truth was bound to surface. Should. She quoted her mama often about truth.

He opened the truck door for her then rolled onto the main highway and cracked the windows. "We forgot to buy a gallon of cider."

The cider could wait. The truth couldn't. "I—" The sound of a pop, then another cut her off, and Colt frowned.

"Hold on. I think a tire blew." He veered off the empty highway onto the shoulder. Nothing but woods on either side. Georgia's stomach roiled.

"Colt." She grabbed his arm, panic pushing pause on her confession.

He laid his hand over hers. "It'll be okay. I need to look." He squeezed her hand. "But slump in your seat a little, just in case." Colt jumped out of the truck and rounded to the passenger side to inspect. Suddenly, he whipped his attention to Georgia. "Get—"

Pop!

A bullet slammed into her door. She shrieked and dived onto the driver's-side floorboard, her chest tightening and her heart racing.

Pop!

Pop!

Pop!

"Colt!" she screamed, unable to see, and all she heard were the sounds of gunfire and metal crunching. Was Colt safe? Had he been injured? What if...what if the shooter killed him?

Her stomach spasmed and sweat broke out over her flushed skin. All she could do was pray.

"Stay down, Georgia!"

Thankfully, his voice reached her ears, but that didn't mean he wasn't hurt. What if he was hurt and the adrenaline was keeping him going? When it crashed he could bottom out, bleed out and die.

Her roiling stomach threatened to retch.

Another sound of gunfire.

Colt cried out, and spots formed in Georgia's vision.

The door opened, and pain washed over Colt's face. "We gotta move. Now."

Georgia's head buzzed and dizziness overtook her. Then she blinked and saw his shoulder was covered in crimson. "You've...you've been shot!"

"Georgia," he said calmly, "focus on my eyes. Breathe. I'm going to be okay."

But how could he know this? He wasn't a doctor!

Colt wrapped his good arm around her and tugged her from the vehicle. "We can't barrel out of this. He's in the trees. Our only chance is to use the truck as cover and roll down the ditch and into the woods on the other side of the road."

"What if he follows?"

"It's a good possibility, but we'll have a big head start."

Another bullet rammed into the windshield. Georgia's brain wouldn't signal her to move, but she had to in order to stay alive and get Colt some help. She forced herself to speak. "Okay."

"Stay down but run hard. Now!" Colt yanked on her hand, and they darted across the road. A bullet hit the pavement by her foot and broke up the concrete.

Colt dived onto her body, and they crashed to the ground, rolling down the grassy hill to the ditch, where they abruptly halted. Colt grimaced and touched his wounded shoulder; the blood coated his fingers and he wiped it on his pants.

Georgia's legs turned to water, but Colt hauled her upright and toward the trees for cover. Pine needles and branches crunched under their feet. They hurdled logs and pushed their way through brush, and his shirt grew redder. Her breathing labored.

"This should lead us back toward the orchard and straight into the cornfield, if I'm right." He continued his fast pace, dragging Georgia along.

"Corn *maze*. They turn it into a fifteen-acre corn maze during October and early November!" Fear gripped her by the throat. What if they couldn't find their way out? What if they were trapped in there with the killer? Every horrible nightmare raced through her mind, and there was no time for thought replacement.

"Georgia, don't slow down on me now!"

She didn't want to slow down. A killer might be right on them.

A bullet splintered bark above her head. Her mouth opened to scream, but nothing came out. Whoever was after them wasn't playing around.

Colt zigzagged through the trees until they reached the tall golden cornstalks.

Georgia could feel herself shutting down. Colt was bleeding. He might be dying. The killer was on their heels. And they might get lost inside the maze.

Another bullet brought her back to life when it hit the ground by her feet. She bolted with Colt into the cornstalks and ran down the rows, tripping over clods of dirt and dried silks.

The stalks were too tall and thick to see over or past. They were running blindly.

Row after row.

Georgia's heart beat in her throat and threatened to explode in her chest; her lungs burned and her palm was slick with sweat inside Colt's, but he kept a grip on her and didn't let her stumble and fall. Under his breath, he muttered a prayer for guidance.

Then he halted, and Georgia almost tripped over him. He put his index finger on his lips to signal her to silence, but her breathing felt louder than a siren. "Do you have your phone?" He pointed to her purse.

"No, I had it out checking my texts before the tire popped."

He cocked his head and listened. Cornstalks rustled in the breeze. A kid hollered in the distance. It was nearly five, and the sun was setting. What would they do in the dark?

Don't panic. God's grace is sufficient. What was the

worst that could happen? They could die. Colt could die! She could not live with that. *What evidence did she have to support that thought?* Up until now, Colt had been brave and gotten them out of trouble. He hadn't been hurt previously. He could lead them out of this. Guides came through every thirty minutes to lead lost sojourners back to the farm. They wouldn't be lost forever. But could they keep out of the killer's grip?

"I don't hear footsteps," Colt whispered. "I think we should go left." He held her with steady strength and quietly led her in the direction he felt they needed to go.

There were people all in this thing; voices were echoing in the distance. Would a killer take a chance on shooting only to risk hurting someone else and dragging more charges down on him? If he was desperate… he might. And with so much land, hearing guns fire was as regular as hearing a bird chirp.

A spray of dirt flew into the air about four feet from them.

Colt ducked and dragged her as they hauled it down the row, zigging and zagging—until they hit a dead end in the maze.

Georgia's knees buckled. "We can't turn back. Might be waiting on us. He's serious."

"And calculated. He followed us to the orchard—but I never saw the tail. He slashed our tires knowing it would cause a fast flat, and then he forced us into the maze. He knows the lay of the land, the timing of traffic—or lack of, in this case. He's prepared. Definitely local."

Colt wasn't easing her anxiety.

"We have to cut through and make our own path, Georgia. It's the only way."

"I don't know…" Her shirt stuck to her back, and she

was shaking so bad she might come out of her skin. *God, I need Your grace to get me through this!*

"Do you trust me?"

"It's not about trust, Colt." She trusted him implicitly, and while she was terrified she might die, her anxiety was over him. She was afraid he might die and she hated to admit it, but she cared about him! She hadn't wanted to. But she did.

He clutched his shoulder. "You're right. We can't go back." He raked a hand through his now-damp hair. "Look at me. Right in my eyes. Breathe. In. Out."

She focused on the intensity in his eyes, the warmth, the hope, the security and strength that pulsed through them, but the shadow of blood on his shoulder distracted her.

"In. Out. We are going to make it. God is going to make a way. Breathe. God is in control. He knows where we are, and He knows the way out. In. Out."

Gradually, her chest released and she could breathe. Circulation returned to her hands and feet. Her heart rate leveled out.

In the distance, voices grew louder and the panic grew quieter, giving her the mental focus she needed to think rationally. But Colt needed medical attention. Color had washed out of his cheeks.

Whistle.

Whistle! She reached into her purse and pulled out the whistle on her key ring. The killer wouldn't be able to identify the source of the whistle, but if a guide or group of people were close by, they'd know someone might be lost and come for them. It was their only hope.

She held it up, and Colt grinned. "I could kiss you, Georgia Jane Maxwell!"

Before this debacle, she might have let him. But now he'd been shot. Proving his line of work was dangerous and he could be wounded—or worse—at any moment.

Kissing was out. And if the whistle idea didn't work, it wouldn't matter.

They'd be dead.

EIGHT

Darkness had settled well over two hours ago. The brilliant whistle trick had worked and brought guides to shuffle them out of the maze. The sheriff's office, his team and the medics had been called. Colt had been grazed and needed about four stitches, but ibuprofen had helped with the pain.

Georgia, however, hadn't said more than two words after she found out he was okay and it was only a flesh wound. Right now, he sat at her farm table, thrumming his fingers while she pulled yet another apple pie from the oven. She'd been baking for half the evening. He thought swinging her by to check on her dogs would help her, and it had, but the minute she walked in the door, she went straight to the kitchen and shut down emotionally. She'd been so brave since her earlier attacks, but this one had put the nail in the coffin. What about it was different?

He'd been wounded.

"Georgia. I don't know how many more times I can say it, but I'm fine. I'm going to be okay."

She removed her oven mitts and shook her head. "You don't know that. You go into the line of fire every day.

You can't say you'll be okay when you don't know the future." She laid the mitts on the counter and leaned over the kitchen sink.

He rose from the table and casually entered her personal space, laying his hands on her shoulders. "Georgia, I know the risks involved. I'm trained. I can protect you. And I promise you I won't stop fighting for you, to keep you safe and get you back to a normal life again."

"I wish for a normal life, Colt. But mine is a far cry from that."

He carefully turned her toward him, hurting with her. He framed her face. "I guess we can't define normal, can we?"

"No," she murmured. She slipped her arms around his waist, burrowing into him. Her fruity shampoo scent wafted into his nostrils as the cap of her hair tickled his neck. The way she leaned into him for support tempted him to stay on past his six weeks if necessary, and he only hoped Atlanta would wait until this last case was closed.

But Georgia…she wasn't a case to be closed. She was much more than an assignment. More than a task. *God, help me. I'm barely holding on to my resolve—to what I know is the safest path to keep my heart protected.*

Georgia pulled back, and her eyes were watery. "I was going to tell you earlier before we got caught in the corn maze. I lied to you," she whispered on shaky breath.

Lied? "About what?"

"When we broke up. You asked me if I ever loved you at all. I said I didn't know. I lied. I loved you. I loved you with everything in me." A tear slipped down her cheek, and every logical reason blew out the door of his mind like a gale of wind.

He brushed away a hair stuck to her tearstained cheek and met her lips with delicate anticipation. His fingers slid into the strands hanging from the messy knot on her head, and a velvety gasp escaped her, fueling him to lean into the kiss with more intensity. She met it with equal zeal, her hands sliding up his back, then her fingers curling into the hair at the nape of his neck. A familiar gesture, but it evoked new emotions. The desire to protect her, to meet her needs and expectations. A soaring in his chest expanded his lungs as if he could kiss her forever, without the need to inhale a single breath.

There was no height or depth he wouldn't travel, no path he wouldn't carve to ensure she was safe, secure and stable. He wanted it for her so badly he tasted it in this cinnamon-and-vanilla-flavored kiss. It consumed him in ways he never fathomed and gave him a confidence he'd never even experienced.

The words were there on the tip of his tongue touching hers begging to be spoken—to offer up his devotion to her—but a knock on the door jarred a dose of sense into him and he broke the kiss, focusing his attention on the noise from the porch.

"I'll get it," he said in a husky voice. As he approached the door, he still tasted her on his lips, but the courage he'd felt two seconds ago deflated like a weeks-old helium balloon.

She hadn't said *love*—she'd said *loved*.

Their feelings were in the past, but there was undeniable chemistry and attraction. That, coupled with overwhelming emotion from the tense circumstances and nostalgia…a kiss was bound to happen at some point.

But he couldn't shake it. He was like an intoxicated man needing the drunk tank to sober up. He tossed her a heady glance before opening the door. Georgia's cheeks were flushed and her eyes glazed with the satisfaction of a good kiss.

But was that all it was for her? Was that all it was for him?

"McCoy! Open the door."

He blinked out of his stupor to see Ryan Sedgwick. What was Chance's alibi doing here? Warning bells rang. His gun was on his hip, so he cracked open the door. He wasn't taking any chances. "Ryan."

"Hey, Colt. I went by the station, and Sheriff told me you were staying out here at Georgia's place. I need to talk to you while I have the courage." Ryan's shifty eyes and jittery stance revealed hesitation and a dose of nervousness. If Colt made him wait, he might lose the moxie.

"No offense, Ryan, but I'm gonna have to pat you down before you come in."

"I understand." He raised his arms. "I heard about the attacks on Georgia. Daisy told my wife y'all had been to the orchard today and someone shot you in the corn maze."

"Yep." Colt searched him, finding him clean. Surely if he was the attacker he wouldn't be dumb enough to try something, but he might be here to mine information. Colt would tread lightly. "Georgia, he's clear. You good with him coming inside?"

She nodded and Ryan entered. "Sorry about all that's happenin' to ya."

"Thanks. You want a piece of fresh apple pie?"

Ryan jammed his hands in his pockets. "No, thank you. I appreciate it, though. I'm here because the truth is I lied all those years ago, and I was going to lie again, but it's not the Christian thing to do. I've been going to church the past few years, and some things in my life have changed."

Seemed like lying and coming clean was the theme of the night. "What part did you lie about?" Colt asked.

"About Chance being with us all night. He was for like twenty minutes, and then he said he had something to do and he'd catch up with us later." He massaged the back of his neck. "The next morning he called and told me if anyone asked where he was, he was with us all night."

"Where was he really?" Colt's stomach knotted.

"I don't know. He wouldn't say then or over the years when we asked. But his daddy gave me and Joey each ten thousand dollars as a college scholarship from his firm two days after Jared died."

Hush money. Whatever Chance did that night, he'd confessed to his dad—who made sure one of the best attorneys was around to bail him out of trouble.

Had Ryan unknowingly accepted blood money?

A couple days had passed since they'd been shot at and now, Georgia sat in an uncomfortable chair across from the interview room at the SO.

Yesterday had been spent trying to find out if James Kreger was a legit person who purchased the property at 4214 Pine Road or if he was fictitious and something like a shell corporation had been used to buy the land. Still, there would be red tape to cut through. Who had access to scissors?

Terry Helms, the booster and the president of First Hope Bank & Loan, which happened to be the premiere bank in Magnolia. The team had interviewed him yesterday about illegal recruiting and the property. Naturally, he dismissed it as nothing more than their wild imagination and the need to pin it on someone, but Terry could have easily fudged documents and secured the land under a false name. Colt said they didn't have enough to secure a warrant for his financials, but they'd attempted it anyway. Judge Herron had denied it. But then, Judge Herron hit the back nine with Terry on Saturday mornings.

The prints hadn't come back yet on Jared's watch, and the fibers hadn't turned up anything that would lead them to the location where he'd been murdered. Colt's team had received the video footage of Dandy's carjacking and murder—which Georgia declined to watch, preferring the CliffsNotes after the team viewed it.

The summation was whoever killed Dandy likely killed Harry Benard. The knife wounds were identical and the assailant's stature from the video matched the likeness of the man who attacked Georgia on that Friday night.

The killer had approached the car with a knife and forced Dandy inside. An altercation broke out. Dandy appeared to go on the offensive, but she'd been stabbed and the killer exited the vehicle. He'd worn dark clothes and a solid-colored ball cap. Not one angle had revealed his face. Georgia shivered, thankful she hadn't watched.

The only trace evidence found at Dandy's crime scene were fibers from Wrangler jeans, which could be purchased anywhere by anyone. But due to new information, the MPD was going to look at new angles as well. Their investigations would now overlap.

With the information Ryan Sedgwick had given Monday night, they were going to talk with Chance Leeway again. Ryan had no intentions of admitting to Chance that he ratted him out, but he knew it would probably come to light in further interviews.

Georgia toyed with her picture key chain. Wyatt and Doc sitting on her porch steps. While she missed them terribly, even after visiting them yesterday, she decided to let Dr. Reed kennel them for a few more days. She couldn't risk her babies getting purposely hurt or indirectly finding themselves in the crosshairs. Dr. Reed had a huge area for play, and they would have fun with other dogs, but she wanted them with her and knew they'd want to be with their person. Sometimes decisions were hard but for the best.

Like the decision not to pursue anything in the present with Colt. Monday night's kiss circled back to the forefront of her heart. That kiss had revealed more than passion. More than the need to connect. It was full of hope and promise.

And then she remembered the lung-crushing panic as his shoulder had bled from a gunshot wound. This time he was safe. But what about next time? Or the next? Maybe not today or tomorrow, but next year or five years from now.

She couldn't do it. Couldn't take the risk. Revealing the truth of the past was the right thing. Kissing him hadn't been. Because all it gave was false hope and a watery promise. Georgia had been protecting herself and him all those years. She'd done it the wrong way— with a lie. But by not getting involved now, meaning no more kissing, she was protecting them both again. Her from triggers and a life saddled with constant anxiety, and Colt from being tied to all that entailed. Talking her off one ledge in the woods was nothing compared to dealing with her worry and fearfulness over him and his job on a daily basis.

Her phone buzzed. Charlie. Since the drama had unfolded, he'd absorbed her responsibility of the classifieds so she could focus on the big story. She read the text and laughed.

Why do so many people want John Deere equipment?

"What's so funny?" Colt asked and entered the room, looking like a solid ten. Gray dress pants and a royal blue button-down that brought out his eyes. He'd rolled the sleeves and held a dollar in his hand as he approached the vending machine. He was not helping her remain strong.

"Farm equipment."

He smirked as the machine ate his money and coughed out an oat and honey granola bar. "What have you been in here thinking? I know your mind's been turning something over."

The kiss. The one neither of them had mentioned had built a thin wall of tension between them, but not enough to keep them from working together or discussing the case. But it needed to be talked about—as in talking about it not happening again. It would only end in more heartbreak.

She'd lead with other thoughts. "Chance's secret."

"Me too." He opened the green package and offered her one of the crunchy bars.

She accepted, and her stomach growled in an anticipation. "A phone call to Jared doesn't make him a murderer. But what he did after the call was obviously worth ten grand each to Ryan Sedgwick and Joey March. Still might not make him a murderer, but he's guilty of something he doesn't want discovered. Not then and not now."

Colt smiled and broke off a piece of granola bar. Crumbs fell to the floor. "Go on, Detective."

Heat ballooned in her cheeks, but she was on a roll. "It's possible he didn't do anything criminal the night of Jared's death, but because of his threats, he needed a solid alibi to prevent him from becoming a suspect. His college career was about to take off, and that kind of heat could have kept him from being accepted to Ole Magnolia. And with Jared out of the picture, Chance was good enough to play QB. So maybe twenty grand was a logical idea to a shady criminal attorney."

Colt's amusement showed in the quirk of his right eyebrow and the flicker in his eyes. "Done?"

"For now."

He chuckled. "You present a solid idea. How about we go see for ourselves? Have us a little chat with him. Shake him up on his own turf."

Georgia broke off another bite. "Yes, because here's the deal. If the money was given in exchange for a solid alibi so the police wouldn't look hard at Chance, then why didn't he come clean to his friends about what he was actually doing the night Jared died? If it wasn't criminal, why continue to keep it a secret?"

Colt cocked his head. "You have something there, Detective. Definitely onto something."

His faith in her and the fact he truly listened didn't help her in the feelings department. "Thanks. But I know we have to cover all our bases. Chance is only one. The recruiting ring is another. Third base—any other enemies of Jared's?"

"Everyone loved him, Georgia. You know that."

"Do I? Jared kept secrets before he died. The money. The concert tickets. Not to mention he'd been extra irritated at Amber, and they usually got along famously."

"Siblings fight."

"Yeah, but once she said she wished they hadn't been fighting. That things might have been different. I thought she meant their relationship, but what if she meant something else, Colt? I'm only bringing it up now because nothing has been as it seems. Fifteen years ago, no one thought for a second it would revolve around illegal football recruiting, but here we are."

Colt ran his tongue across his upper teeth. "Well, let's talk to her again, then we'll talk to Chance."

Twenty minutes later, they arrived at Amber's.

Amber opened up, serious-faced, but then she beamed at Colt and hugged him. "I'm glad it's you investigating, Colton."

"Thanks. I'm doing everything I can."

She invited them inside her cozy living room. Colt and Georgia perched on the love seat.

"Karen and Dad said you'd reopened the case and had new evidence. I'm guessing that's why you're here and to get my story from that night."

They made a few minutes of small talk then got down to business.

"Where were you that night that he died?" Colt asked.

"Grounded. At home." She shrugged and half laughed.

Georgia hated to bring up uncomfortable memories, but... "Amber, I told Colt what you said. About how if you and Jared hadn't been fighting, things might have been different. What exactly did you mean?"

Amber ran her hand across her face and slumped on

the couch, shaking her head. "Seventeen-year-old girls do dumb things. You know that, Georgia."

Did she ever.

"Go on," Colt encouraged.

"Remember Scott Hazer?" Amber asked.

"The drug dealer who hung around the high school?" He'd only been about three years older than them, but he was trouble with a capital *T.* "What about him?"

"Well, back then he was just a good-looking bad boy and…" She tossed her hands up. "I thought underneath that tough exterior he was a sweet guy who needed some self-esteem."

Colt raised his eyebrows.

"In my defense, I was seventeen and stupid, and he was great-looking." Amber's cheeks turned pink. Seemed like she still had fond memories of him. Scott had been handsome—still was. Occasionally, Georgia spotted him around town. Back then, he'd given her the creeps lurking around school dances and football games.

"Connect the dots, please," Colt insisted.

"I went out with him a few times, and Jared caught us together. He warned me to stay away, and he had words with Scott to leave me alone. But the Friday night before he died, he caught us talking after the football game. Jared made me leave and wait in his car, but I saw them arguing, and Scott pushed him. Jared didn't tell me what they said, but told me Scott wasn't going to bother me again, and if he found out I was initiating contact, he'd tell Dad."

Georgia's gut clenched, and she caught Colt's eye. "Did Jared threaten Scott concerning the drugs he peddled?"

Amber's eyes grew wide, and her face blanched. "I didn't hear him say that."

"But you must have thought so if you felt like y'all's arguing over Scott might have been the difference between him living and dying. You think Scott killed him, don't you?" Georgia asked.

"I don't know. I don't think so…but I can't say it hasn't crossed my mind."

"We're going to look into it now," Colt said. "Anything else I need to know?"

She shook her head.

Georgia's gut wasn't so sure Amber wasn't still hiding something. She should have come forward with this back then, but she'd been a scared girl afraid of her parents and what they might do if they found out she was seeing a known troublemaker and drug dealer. "You sure?"

"Georgia, if I knew who killed Jared, I'd tell you. I'd have told the cops. But I don't know anything for certain."

"Did you see Scott again?" Georgia asked. "After Jared died."

Amber's eyes watered. "Yes. A week after he died, Scott got in touch with me. He was oddly quite comforting and kind. No underlying motives or anything. It obviously went nowhere. But I do see him from time to time, and I don't know, it seems like…maybe regret in his eyes that things hadn't worked out."

Or that he killed her brother. If only she knew what Jared and Scott argued about and what would keep Scott from attempting to see Amber again. Even if they interviewed Scott, they'd never know if he was telling the truth.

"Thanks for your time. It was good seeing you again.

I hate it was under these circumstances." Colt hugged her, and they let themselves out.

"Chance Leeway, Coach Flanigan and now Scott Hazer all look equally good for the crime," Georgia said as they backed out of the drive. "I had no idea Amber even had a crush on Scott. She should have told me."

"She knew you'd worry," he said softly. "You were always a worrier."

Colt hadn't meant it to sound negative, but it had been a negative thing in her life and in his. It continued to hold her back from things she might want in life, and it controlled her more than she'd admit. The battle was never ending.

"I'll get Scott Hazer's address and we'll drop by. In the meantime, let's go see Chance and break the news that we know he lied about his alibi."

A storm was brewing, but this time, they had the upper hand.

Didn't they?

NINE

Southern High was located in the southern half of Magnolia. The Tigers had been a good team, but never as good as Courage High—and maybe that was because someone at Courage High was poaching players. Were all of Coach's wins due to cheating instead of growing talented players? Was it Coach who was poaching, or was he truly in the dark about the falsified addresses?

Colt pulled into visitor parking, and he and Georgia exited the vehicle. Aside from coaching, Chance taught Algebra I and II.

They entered the school office, and he showed his creds to the secretary. She told them Chance was in his planning period in his office on A Hall. The school smelled of bleach and sweaty boys. The tile floors had recently been buffed, and only a few black sole scuffs were visible in spots.

Now that Harry Benard had passed, Chance would more than likely move up to head coach. Better pay. Better position. Colt wasn't so sure Chance had killed Harry, and even if he did—they strongly suspected whoever killed him also killed Dandy. What would Chance's motive be for killing her? He had nothing to do with an illegal recruiting ring fifteen years ago, and that was what she'd been looking into. Unless what happened over a decade ago could link somehow to Chance and his secret.

The hall was quiet. Banners hung above the lockers, paying respects to Coach Benard. He'd clearly been beloved. Voices coming from Chance's office echoed in the hall, and Colt put his arm out to halt Georgia from entering.

"Just keep your mouth shut," Chance said with venom. "My dad takes care of you, doesn't he? Have you ever done one day of time? No. And you won't unless your lips loosen."

"Don't threaten me, Chance. I don't need your dad or you. Remember that. But you need me."

Colt and Georgia shared a wide-eyed gaze. That voice sounded vaguely familiar. Colt inched closer to the door to get a peek at who was in the room.

No. Way.

He whispered, "It's Scott Hazer."

Georgia gaped. Colt swept into the office. "Hey, sorry for coming by unannounced. Didn't mean to overhear, but—"

Scott charged Colt and pummeled him to the ground, obviously having spotted his gun and badge on his belt. Georgia shrieked outside the door, and Colt jumped to his feet—his ribs were gonna feel that later. "Don't you go anywhere," he barked at Chance and tore out of the office. Georgia was getting to her feet. "You okay?"

"Yeah, go!"

Scott was halfway down the hall, the heels of his shoes squeaking along the tile flooring as he headed for the gymnasium. Colt gave chase. Scott burst through the exit doors that led outside to the football field as Colt entered the gym.

Colt drew his weapon and hollered for him to stop, but as usual, criminals ignored law enforcement's commands and he kept on trucking toward the football field. Thankfully, Colt hadn't given up long-distance running, and he gained on Scott until he reached him and tackled him like it was a Friday night, his gun slipping from his hand.

Scott elbowed him in the chest and went for the Sig Sauer. Colt lost his breath but grappled for the gun lying on the field. Colt retrieved it and growled under his breath, "You're under arrest for assaulting an officer of the law. Nice going, idiot." He pulled his cuffs and secured Scott in the bracelets. He called in backup, and within eight minutes they'd arrived and hauled Scott into the back seat of the squad car.

Colt met Georgia by the back doors. "Chance?"

"In his office. But he called his dad, so you know. I stuck around to make sure he wouldn't run. I was worried about you."

"I'm right as rain." His shoulder throbbed and burned from having to manhandle Scott, but he refrained from sharing that with Georgia. It would only ramp up her worry. Colt wiped the sweat from his brow. "Chance might be dangerous. You should have gotten out of there. If you're going to fret, fret over that."

She pursed her lips and touched his shoulder. "You might have torn a stitch. You're bleeding."

So much for her not distressing over him. "I'll look at it when I get time. Come on."

She opened her mouth to protest but remained silent and followed him inside and back to Chance's office.

Chance sat smugly in his office chair, as if he hadn't been caught talking suspiciously to a known drug dealer. "Well, I can bring you in the back of a squad car or you can come discreetly on your own, but we're definitely going to have a conversation," Colt said. "We know you lied about your alibi. One of your buds came forward. We also know about the ten thousand your dad paid Ryan and Joey in exchange for their lies."

Chance didn't miss a beat, didn't even flinch. "That was a scholarship from his firm and you can't prove otherwise. The paperwork will show it's legit. You're gonna have to do better than that."

This guy got all under Colt's skin. "Maybe. But that doesn't explain the fact you lied and said you were at the Dairy Freeze all night when we know you weren't." Colt motioned for him to stand. "Don't try anything stupid, Leeway. Go straight to the station and be thankful I'm allowing this courtesy."

Chance narrowed his eyes and collected his keys and wallet.

Within fifteen minutes, Colt was in the interview room with Scott Hazer. Rhett sat in with him. Georgia and Mae watched from behind the glass. Poppy was in with Chance. She knew football and how to work an arrogant suspect.

Scott's jaw hardened as he rubbed his dark scruffy cheeks, hair disheveled. He smelled like stale cigarette smoke and sweat. This was the guy Amber had crushed on? She'd spoken of regretful eyes, but the only thing radiating from Scott's glare was belligerence and disgust.

"I'd like to talk to you about Jared Toledo." Colt tented his fingers on the metal table.

"Jared Toledo is dead and I didn't do it."

"I'm not saying you did." Yet. "But we know you had a thing with Amber Wilcox and Jared didn't like it. The two of you tangled, and I want to know how mad you were over it."

Scott licked his bottom lip and folded his arms across his chest, letting his glare bounce between Rhett and Colt.

Colt had overheard Chance talking about his dad being Scott's lawyer. New approach. "Chance Leeway and his father have a lot of connections and money. If Chance is involved in Jared's murder, they'll want to find a fall guy. And it's obvious that the two of you have history and some sort of relationship now—likely drug use. His daddy may be your lawyer who has, and can, get you out of jams, but he's Chance's father. Who do you think he's going to defend first and fiercest?"

"I'd have to go with Chance, but what do I know?" Rhett asked. "What's that saying about blood being thicker than water?"

"That is the saying," Colt returned and grinned. He and Rhett chatted up the chances nonchalantly while Scott squirmed. They had this down to an art form. They had nothing to lose if he talked or not, but he would sit here for hours and had everything to lose. Once it sank in, he'd talk—at least a little. They always did.

"But who knows," Rhett added. "Maybe you're more like a son to Reggie Leeway than Chance. I wonder if you're in the will. I imagine it's a substantial amount of money."

"What, maybe a few mil?" Colt asked.

"Oh, at least," Rhett said. "And the house. I hear it's a really nice house."

And that did the trick.

Scott haltingly released his clenched jaw and leaned forward on the table. "Look, I didn't have a beef with Jared. I get I was no good for his sister. Whatever. We got into it and yeah, I muscled him some, but he said he had proof of me doing something...not so legal, and if I went near her, he'd give it to the cops."

Colt's gut clenched. "What did you do about that?"

"I called in a favor from Chance. I wanted the camera and the film or SD card or whatever. Chance owed me."

"Why?"

Scott shook his head. "Doesn't matter why. He owed, and the favor was getting me that proof." Scott wasn't as stupid as he looked. No way Jared would let him near a camera. If Scott was telling the truth, which Colt believed he was, Chance had a better shot of lifting the evidence. He could get in closer contact.

"So you could continue seeing Amber."

"The photos had nothing to do with her. I don't need nobody having pictures of me. Holding stuff over me. No proof. No worries. I didn't kill Jared. I can't say what Chance did or didn't do."

How did any of this connect to illegal recruiting or Georgia's attacks? It was obvious whoever came after Georgia was steamed about the evidence that linked to illegal recruiting and that led back to Dandy's original inquiry to what was going on in the Courage High district and Ole Magnolia University. Could two separate crimes be going on at one time?

"I'll be straight with you, Scott. I don't care about your drug dealing. Everyone knows about it. That's between you and the local police. I'm here to find out who killed Jared, and what I have is Chance's crumbled alibi and the need to know where he was when Jared died.

Now, I have him linked to you and Jared as well. Where were you that night?"

He laughed. "I barely know where I was yesterday. But I know where Chance Leeway was the night Jared died."

"Where?"

"Met Jared at the Magnolia Motel to get the evidence."

"Did he get it?"

Scott leaned back in his chair. "Yeah. He broke the camera and the SD card all right there for me to see. Like a good boy." He snorted. "Why would I kill Jared? I got what I wanted."

"Why did Chance tell you to keep your mouth shut?"

Scott splayed his hands in front of him. "Guess he knew we might be right here chatting like this."

Colt stood. "Sit tight." He left Rhett with Scott and met up with Mae and Georgia in the other room.

Georgia pointed to the glass. "I believe him."

"He's still hiding something and I don't trust him," Mae countered.

Georgia rubbed her chin. "Let's connect the obvious dots. Scott dealt drugs. He had a connection to Chance that neither will cough up. It's likely drugs—possibly even performance-enhancing drugs. Chance owes him, and it's probably over illegal substances."

"He might have owed Scott money for drugs," Mae offered.

"Exactly," Georgia said. "Scott has Chance meet up with Jared and they choose the Magnolia, which we know Scott dealt from often. He may have even been in one of the rooms waiting on the photos. The altercation could have taken place that night at the motel. We know Jared's body was relocated after his death. But by Scott or Chance?"

Colt was on the same page as the women. "The phone call from Chance to Jared the night he was working out at the school was likely to get him to meet. But it had to be a bogus lure. Jared wouldn't have met up with Chance to give him pictures willingly. How did he get him to the Magnolia?"

"And how does this possibly link to my attacks and the illegal recruiting?" Georgia asked.

That was a great question. It was possible that Georgia's attacks were to silence her about the illegal recruiting. Which opened up the case and led to Jared's murder investigation—the catalyst but not a direct link.

Gerald and Karen had denied that Jared accepted a bribe to go to Ole Magnolia. But Jared was secretive about the money and concert tickets. Could he have bribed Scott or Chance for the money and tickets? Was the photo of Scott dealing drugs to Chance?

"Has Poppy gotten anything from Chance?"

Mae shook her head. "Just football talk. The guy is smart. He knows how to evade incriminating questions. And his dad showed up about five minutes ago. He's in there with him."

Great. "I'll take a crack at him anyway. We have history. And I have Scott's story. That ought to give me some leverage."

Poppy stood as Colt entered, and he gave her a chin nod—the signal to leave them inside alone.

"I'm gonna get a coffee. Anyone want one?" She didn't wait for them to respond. "Okay, just me then."

Reggie Leeway eyed Colt like a hawk about to strike a lone kitten. Colt was no helpless fluff ball. He was a unit chief, and he'd gone toe to toe with slimy lawyers like Reggie before.

"I've talked to Scott." No point holding back. He relayed Scott's story, except the fact Scott refused to admit what the favor was in exchange for. "We know you were buying drugs from Scott and you owed him."

Reggie laid a hand on Chance's forearm, and Chance remained silent. But to Colt, that was a clear sign indicating the favor was linked to Chance and personal drug use.

"Are you charging him? If not, you have to let him go," his father said.

"I want to know your side of this story, Chance." Technically, he could hold him up to forty-eight hours, and Reggie knew it. If it came to that, he would. Colt stared at Reggie with steel in his eyes, daring him to test him.

Reggie nodded to Chance and gave him permission to speak.

"Scott asked for a favor. I complied. I called Jared that Saturday night. You already know this. I asked him to meet me. I didn't want to come to the school, because I knew his coach was in his office. He'd been talking to him when I called."

"Meet you for what?" What was the ploy to coax him into meeting?

"I'd popped off the night before—you know that. I offered to buy him some fries and a drink at Rascal's." Right across from the Magnolia Motel. "It'd be easy to get it and then deliver it to Scott."

"Scott was at the motel waiting on you?"

"He was supposed to be, but I think one of his friends

didn't show up, and when I met up with him it was at his house."

"What happened at Rascal's?"

"We ate fries at about nine thirty. We talked football, and I apologized for being a jerk. When he went to the bathroom, I checked his jacket for the camera. No go."

"So how did you get it?"

"I was working on a plan B that would get me to his house so I could dig around his room. But on our way out, I saw it in his back seat along with an Aerosmith T-shirt. I'd heard he scored front-row tickets, and I told him I didn't buy it and wanted to see for myself. When he dug around in his duffel bag for them, I lifted the camera."

"Did you look at the pictures?"

Chance looked at his dad. He again nodded. "No. It was empty."

Scott said Chance broke it right in front of him. Surely he wouldn't be dumb enough not to look first. "Scott said—"

"I know what Scott said. I went to the 7-Eleven on the corner of his block and bought an SD card. He was high when he called, so I had a fifty-fifty shot. I broke the camera and disk, and he bought it. But the original card was never there."

"Where was Jared when you last saw him and what time?"

"It was about ten when I left the parking lot at Rascal's. Alice Parker was working the night shift and saw us. Ask her. She saw me get into my car and leave. Jared was sitting in his when I drove away. What happened after Rascal's, I honestly don't know."

Colt put the missing pieces together. When Jared

turned up dead, Chance admitted to his dad he'd been involved with a drug dealer and told him what happened. His dad then had him use Joey and Ryan as alibis. Not only to protect him from being a murder suspect but to hide the drugs. No college would have him if either of those things were on his record. Not to mention it would tarnish Chance's name and their family reputation. And for Scott's silence, Mr. Leeway became his lawyer— probably pro bono.

But Alice Parker had been interviewed fifteen years ago when she worked as the secretary for Gerald's used auto dealership. Anyone who might have had any contact with him was spoken with, and Jared had worked a few afternoons at the dealership in the office. Colt didn't re-call her mentioning that she saw Jared the night he died.

Colt wanted to review her statement again.

"You're free to go."

Georgia sat across from Colt and the team at Jose's— best tacos in town. The lunch crowd had jam-packed the place. Noise, laughter, sizzling fajitas and clanking dishes suffused the atmosphere.

After Chance and his father left, the team had gone over old statements, more specifically Alice Parker's. She noted Jared being a wonderful young man who worked occasionally for Gerald at the dealership and she often interacted with him, but nothing revealed she'd seen him the night of the murder.

After ordering their meals and pouring personal dishes of salsa, Georgia couldn't keep silent.

"I've known Alice my whole life. Why didn't she mention seeing Jared and Chance the night he died?"

She dipped her chip in the salsa, and a burst of cilantro and tomato sent her in for another.

"I don't think Chance is lying. He knows we'll talk to Alice for corroboration. He expects her to admit to seeing him." Colt mixed cheese dip with his salsa and scooped a hefty bite.

"Y'all have known this lady your whole lives, but what do you really know about her?" Rhett asked as he helped himself to more queso.

"Basics. Married. Has a son younger than us by a year or so." Colt sipped his sweet tea—no lemon. "Georgia, you've stuck around town—what do you know?"

She wiped her hands on the black linen napkin spread across her lap. "Personally—not a lot. She works for the clerk's office now. Has for some time. She goes to Hope Church, and she heads up the book drive every spring. Susan did a piece on her and the drive last year."

"We need to talk to her. Find out why she held back pertinent information."

"You only hide important information if you have something to hide. What is Alice hiding?" Georgia asked.

"Maybe a drug habit. She might have been one of Scott's clients and even in the photos Jared had on him. He could have told her about the pictures. Or maybe she owes Reggie Leeway a favor for something and kept quiet to protect Chance—but then why would Chance offer her up now?" Colt asked.

"Because he was caught. Might as well let her admit it now."

Laughter interrupted their conversation.

Coach Flanigan, Terry Helms and Sunny Wilkerson entered the establishment like old friends, cracking jokes and sporting mile-wide grins.

Chance and his friends had already proven that buddies would lie for one another. Were these three partnering up together to hide the illegal recruiting ring? Did one of them kill Dandy? Attack Georgia? Kill Jared?

Had one of them shot Colt? A jolt of adrenaline rushed through her, and her skin crawled as if ants were underneath it. In a flash her appetite was gone.

They squeezed into a booth on the far side of the dining area.

"Where are we on those three?" Colt asked as the server brought their entrées. When she left, Poppy crunched into her taco and held up a finger for him to wait. She swallowed and sipped her water. "Sunny Wilkerson appears squeaky clean, but both Tyler Burgess and Moore Thompson—the boys using the false address— work part-time at his outdoor sports equipment store. Nothing wrong with that. Unless the jobs are favors or incentive to play at Courage."

Harry Benard had approached Moore Thompson's mom before he left Courage High for Southern. Same time he probably approached Tyler Burgess's mother— but they hadn't been able to reach her yet to confirm. Did Harry's departure from Courage High have anything to do with the illegal recruitment and falsifying of addresses? "Did you find out how the boys slid by without showing proof of residence and a utility bill or car tag payment?"

"I met with Principal Wiggins. He had no idea, but then, it's the secretaries and administration who handle scanning that info and filing it. He had their files pulled. No proof of residence or any utility bills for these past two years. He's doing a formal inquiry. The boys will be allowed to finish out the year, but without a legit residence, next year they'll have to go back to their rightful district." Poppy scooped her chip in a heap of guacamole. "I figure it'll end up under the rug. Pinned on Coach Harry Benard. It's not enough reason to kill someone."

Georgia agreed. More was at play here. Had to be. "Both boys worked for Sunny Wilkerson. Played for Coach Flanigan. Did they have a connection to Terry Helms, too?"

"We're looking," Mae said. "We've been tracing Pine Road further back than Dandy's list. Looks like she was still working on it when she was murdered."

"And?"

"The land was purchased by the obscure James Kreger sixteen years ago. We pulled school records of athletes seventeen years ago—nothing. All legit addresses. No Pine Road. But the year—" she used air quotes "—'James Kreger' purchased the land, we found two boys who lived in other districts that used the address to play at Courage. Both of them went on to Ole Magnolia with full rides and played ball for Joe Jackson. We contacted the men, but they acted like they didn't know anything about a fake address or illegal recruiting. And we can't squeeze them, because it's possible they didn't know anything about it. They were minors at the time, and those decisions might have been made without their knowledge by a parent."

"Did you contact the parents?" Colt asked.

Mae sighed. "John Rells's father has dementia and his mom has passed on. Carter Wagoner's parents had no comment." Mae rolled her eyes. "We've contacted six more players and families who used that address over the past ten years. 'I have no comment' is the running theme. It's not like we can bring any heat on them to talk. They're not facing any major charges, and I imagine Reggie Leeway is their lawyer and he's let them know not to comment."

"Who did the elusive James Kreger purchase the land from?" Colt asked.

Mae wiped her mouth. "Willard Blake. Owned it for over thirty years. Probably used it as hunting land. But when he got sick, he sold it. Talked to his niece, but she can't say much about the sale other than it happened. He passed not long after."

"Loyalty goes a long way," Colt said. "Coaches are kings, and these players and families will feel as though they owe them. Who knows how big this thing truly is?"

Georgia wondered the same thing. Big enough that people were dying for it. Families may have been threatened to keep their mouths shut, and if they had gotten wind of Dandy's death and Georgia's attacks, they'd believe whoever threatened them would make good on it.

"Any word from the NCAA on Coach Jackson?"

"They're investigating but haven't made a ruling." Rhett finished his sweet tea and tapped his fingers on the table. "I'm going to follow up again. Don't want them getting lax."

Halfway through their meal, Colt leaned in. "I'm going to go rattle a few cages."

What was one more rattle when Georgia had already shaken the cage and gotten it rocking? "Wait." She was scared, intimidated and terrified, but these guys were not going to know it. Even if she was bluffing, they needed to know she wasn't backing down. Jared and Dandy would receive justice. Time to fake being brave. "I'll go with you."

United front.

Colt frowned. "I don't know. If one of them is your attacker, fueling the fire probably isn't wise."

"One of them shot you, and you're not backing down."

"It's my job."

"Well, I don't want them to think they've succeeded in scaring me—even if they have."

Colt held her stare, then conceded. "Understood. Put on a brave face, but leave the rattling of cages to me."

"Fine."

"I mean it, Georgia. No ruffling feathers. You've already got someone molting." He smirked, but his eyes meant business.

What's the worst that could happen? She could make them even madder and they could attack her again. *Can I live with that?* She was living with it now and she trusted Colt to do his job, though she feared he'd get hurt again. *God is my source of strength and my shield. He's my strong tower, and He's my safe place.* She repeated the good thoughts to replace the negative ones all the way to the men's table.

As they approached, the laughter and conversation died down and a mixture of contempt, confusion and annoyance crossed their expressions.

"Hello again," Colt said. "Enjoying lunch?"

"We are," Coach Flanigan said. "Y'all?"

"Definitely. Hey, curious. Which one of y'all owns 4214 Pine Road?"

Coach's eyebrows lifted, Sunny stared at his plate and Terry Helms laughed. "Property ownership is public record, Colt. Not very good investigator skills going for you there."

Colt's jaw ticked. "See, the thing is one of you are

hiding behind James Kreger. Just wondering which one of you it is."

"Financials are a little more difficult to crack into," Terry said over the rim of his sweet tea.

"And you'd know," Georgia blurted. His verbal swing at Colt fired her up. "You are the bank president. I imagine if we dug hard enough, we'd see that the land was purchased with a loan at your bank. You're a booster. You have everything to lose, Terry, if we find out you've been committing fraud and funneling money and false loans through dummy names. You'd be out a job and that nice big house, speed boats—plural—great cars and all the time you spend at the country club are going to fade away."

Well, she hadn't meant to go that far. She dared a peek at Colt. The big vein in his neck was protruding.

Terry's smug smile faded, and a heavy dose of fear filmed his gray eyes. Good. It was high time someone other than Georgia felt afraid. "And if we find out you killed Jared and Dandy and attempted to murder me—you'll spend the rest of your life in a prison cell. Not a country club."

"Whoa, now." He raised his palms in surrender. "I didn't kill or try to kill anyone."

"But you are involved in illegal recruiting."

Colt pinched the bridge of his nose. She was stopping. Right now.

"I'm not," he insisted. "So I suggest you lower your voice and stop making accusations, Miss Maxwell. Or the only one who's going to regret it is you, when I sue you for defamation of character."

Colt stepped in front of Georgia. "I suggest you watch your threat, Mr. Helms. And we'll be seein' you. All of you." He placed his hand firmly on Georgia's lower back and all but shoved her out the front door.

Outside, he threw his hands in the air. "Georgia. Did we not just talk about how to approach those men?"

"He hit you below the belt, Colt. All the fear…it turned to anger and I lost it. I'm sorry."

"Are you?"

"Mostly." She tried a smile, but it didn't hit its mark.

Colt scowled and massaged the back of his neck. "Quit worrying about me. I can take care of myself. If you can't follow my lead, I'm taking you off the case as a consultant. This isn't an episode of *Castle.*"

"I kicked a beehive. Again. I really am sorry."

Colt glanced toward the restaurant. "I hate how it went down, but sometimes you have to be willing to feel the sting to disable the bee and taste the honey. But no more kicks and stings, Georgia. I'm serious."

The team met them outside. "Well, you sure broke up that good ole time in there," Poppy said. "Maybe you scared them enough that they'll make a mistake or give themselves away."

"Or come after Georgia again," Colt said as he jumped in his truck's driver's seat. "If one of them is the killer."

"You say that as if there might be more than one someone." Georgia buckled up.

"I think we have one killer and a handful of potential ones. There are entirely too many folks trying to keep secrets buried. So any one of them may be your attacker."

She'd never thought of someone other than Jared's killer coming after her. Had she messed with an illegal recruiting cash cow, or had she opened up another can of worms? She didn't even want to ask the worst thing that could happen, because she was *not* okay with the results.

* * *

Georgia blinked awake, groggy. She'd been dreaming she was nestled next to a bonfire, roasting hot dogs, then the smoke plumed heavy and she couldn't escape it. Even now it permeated her senses.

Yesterday afternoon and well into the evening, they'd dug into James Kreger. Was he a real person or a fictitious buyer who had purchased the land? Someone had ponied up twenty-five grand to purchase that property. Had Terry Helms skimmed the money from the bank? Taken out a fake loan somehow? It wouldn't have been too hard to pull off as bank president.

They didn't have enough for a warrant. Yet. But Mae and Rhett were working on it while Poppy tried to poke holes in families and get them to talk. Harry Benard was dead, so if he was the threat keeping them quiet, what did they have to fear? Nothing. Which meant he wasn't the threat.

Man, it really did smell like bonfire smoke. So…real.

A warning struck her sleepy thoughts, and she bolted upright.

Orange flames flickered against the window.

Her house was on fire!

TEN

Georgia's heart lurched into her throat as she bolted from the bed to the door. Colt burst inside as she reached for the knob.

"The house is on fire! Let's go," he bellowed and grabbed her hand. Smoke had enveloped the staircase, blinding them. Georgia tripped on the stairs and clung to Colt. When they reached the living room, she bumped into furniture, stubbing her toes and nailing her shins. Sooty air coated her throat and forced coughing. "Down low," Colt said through his own wheezing.

Wood cracked and popped.

A rafter beam groaned then collapsed to the living room floor with a thundering crash. Embers lit the couch ablaze. Georgia fought inside her own skin to get out. Everything was closing in, and it felt like being cooked on broil in a dark oven.

Her lungs squeezed, and she panted and longed for fresh air.

Colt grabbed a blanket from a basket that had yet to be ravaged and draped Georgia as they slithered on their bellies. "Where do we go?" she cried. What if Colt couldn't find a way out? What if he burned alive and she had to watch and hear his screams?

Flames licked up the sides of the house and the ceiling, daring them to escape its scorching anger. It had reached around her entire home like a garrison holding them hostage. Someone must have saturated every inch of her place with gasoline before lighting the match.

Charred wood fell sporadically. It was like playing a game of dodgeball, only instead of being nailed with rubber they'd end up impaled and burned alive.

Colt shielded Georgia. But who was going to shield him?

"Hang on to my shirt or pant leg so we don't get separated. Let's try the other guest room," he said as he led the way on his stomach. "Maybe the back of the house isn't as bad."

If it had been equally engulfed, she and Colt were doomed.

Sweat poured from her face and down her back. This must be what eternity apart from God felt like. Fire and brimstone. So hot she could barely breathe. Her eyes watered and burned. Georgia crawled blind, unable to detect direction. How on earth was Colt able to lead them?

The house hissed and roared like a fire-breathing dragon. Colt had been using the neck of his shirt as a mask, but it didn't ease his hacks and coughs. Georgia's head went fuzzy. The ravenous fire ate up the oxygen with insatiable greed.

Colt ripped the blankets off the twin-size daybed and jerked the mattress from the springs, then shoved it in the door frame, buying them a few moments of time to try to get out the window—flames already swallowed the holly bushes underneath.

Georgia couldn't swallow. Couldn't move.

"I'm going to wrap you in the blankets and toss you out, Georgia. It's your only hope." Colt's voice shook with urgency and dread.

"And what about you? I can't leave you!" She trembled from head to toe as she strained through stinging eyes to see his sooty, sweaty face. A face she'd loved so much. What if he didn't make it out? What if he was burned to ash? What if he passed out from inhaling the smoke before escaping? Her entire body convulsed with terror, and panic ate at the edges of her synapses.

"I'll be right behind you. Promise." He wrapped her in a knit blanket until she felt mummified, then he double coated her with a thick wedding quilt—even her face had been cocooned, leaving her in utter darkness.

Do not panic. You are safe. God is your shield. Your protector. Your rescuer. He walks with you through fire. He'll walk with Colt, too.

"It'll give you some cushion, but I can't promise you won't feel a few bumps. I'm gonna toss you away from the fire. Clench your teeth to keep from biting your tongue."

She nodded in the thick covering to let him know she'd obeyed and was ready, but her heart was about to beat out of her chest, and she was as far from ready as one person could be.

"We have to move fast," he said. "Now." He lifted her into his arms and swung her like a baby. "God, help us. Direct her landing and keep her safe inside the blanket. Like when You were in the fiery furnace—don't let a single flame touch her!"

Then she was flying.

Whooshing.

Hissing.

Popping.

Her body met the ground with a thud that reverberated through every bone, but nothing appeared broken. Were the flames nearby? Coming for her? She couldn't see!

Her fingers and toes tingled as a panic attack revealed its reckoning. Her insides felt like a bull bucking to get out of the stall. She thrashed and rolled, fighting for freedom from the blanket and quilt.

A piercing cry broke through the atmosphere.

Colt! *Oh, God, let him be okay.* But the sound was tormented. Had he succumbed to the flames?

She shoved and pushed until she unfolded from the blankets, her pulse pounding in her temple, and then she spotted Colt rolling on the ground, his blanket on fire.

Utter shock slammed into her, but she quickly grabbed her quilt and ran for him. No. No! She beat out the flames with the quilt before it engulfed him, then dropped to her knees, shaking uncontrollably.

"Colt! Are you burned? Injured?" She touched his sweaty, blackened face. He coughed.

"I'm okay," he groaned, but his scrunched face revealed the pain. "My ankle... I burned my ankle, but I'm fine. Are you?" He pulled to his feet, favoring his right foot over his burned left foot. "Let's go. Too much smoke," he said as he coughed.

Colt had almost died. He was badly burned—worse than he was letting on. She was losing breath. Losing her mind. A full-blown panic attack came on and sank her to the ground.

"Oh, Georgia. Hey. Hey," Colt said and forced her to look at him. "Breathe. You gotta breathe." But she couldn't. Colt had been injured. Twice. And her fear and distress proved she cared more about him than she ever meant to. Ever intended to.

"We have to get to the woods. To fresh air. Look at me and breathe."

She turned away from him and watched in horror as the raging inferno consumed her home. It groaned and protested as it fell to ash, and inside Georgia mourned with it. Where would she go now that her sanctuary was destroyed? A monster had burned her out and isolated her. She'd faked bravado, then gotten indignant and angry over Colt, and one of those men had settled the score. Everything was burned to the ground.

A wintry chill swept over her fevered skin as it dawned on her that the killer had taken enough reckless chances by shooting her inside her home. Now he'd forced her to leave, which gave him more opportunities to kill her in other places.

"Georgia, look at me. Not the house. Look at me." He patted her cheeks and forced her to peer into his eyes, surrounded by dirt and soot and sweat. "Breathe."

She was no help to anyone in this state. But it was out of her control. Colt prayed, stroking her filthy hair and rocking her in his lap, his bad leg sticking out while she fell to a heap against him. At least her dogs were unharmed.

He kissed her forehead and coughed again. "We need help," he said through a strained voice. "You work on breathing." Colt called 911 and his team.

Georgia had lost track of time, but sirens sounded in the distance. The cold case unit arrived, running alongside the paramedics. Firefighters went to work dousing the fire to contain it, but her house was lost.

She was peppered with questions, medical care, oxygen masks. Surrounded by law enforcement and first responders. Everything moved like a whirlwind. And all she could imagine was Colt dying in that fire. He hadn't just risked his life for Georgia—he'd have done this for anyone—strangers. It was his job. He'd chosen this.

"There's a search going on now for evidence or the perpetrator," Rhett said. "If he's in these woods somewhere, we'll find him."

Colt shoved the oxygen mask from his face. "Let's get to work."

"Let's make sure you're cleared to go," Poppy added, and the paramedic frowned and shoved the mask back on Colt's face.

"You're not," the paramedic said.

Georgia sat, stunned. Colt laced his fingers with hers and squeezed. She peered into his compassionate eyes and saw the flicker of emotion that had also been burning since his earlier kiss—a kiss that had cracked open places she purposely kept sealed. It begged for her to swing it open wide. To stop fighting tooth and nail to avoid it. For a moment, she had given in and believed she might be able to do that. Wanted to or she'd never have allowed that kiss.

But it was reasons like this—like him being shot— that she kept herself locked tight. To avoid these triggers and keep this kind of torment at bay.

He'd been burned and could have been injured further or even died.

This was all too much. Her mind replayed what had happened and what could have happened and might happen over and again.

It all ended with Colt dying and her losing her mind. *God, help me. Heal me!*

"My grace is sufficient for thee: for my strength is made perfect in weakness. Most gladly therefore will I rather glory in my infirmities, that the power of Christ may rest upon me."

Second Corinthians 12:9 once again saturated her heart. It had been God alone getting her through these trials. Literally through the fire.

And they had made it out alive. God had used Colt to spare them.

"Georgia, talk to me," Colt said.

"I'm so glad you had a good throwing arm and played football in high school," Georgia breathed, using dry humor to help her cope.

"Me too. I could have thrown you straight into the wall or worse—the fire." Colt winced as they examined his burns. Puckers of red flesh covered his ankle and some of his shin. "I'm sorry. I should have stayed awake. I would have realized we were in trouble sooner."

"Colt, you're a human being. You have to sleep. Do not blame yourself."

"We've cleaned the wounds, but you need to see a doctor," the EMT interrupted.

"I don't want to see a doctor."

The paramedic frowned. "You want it to get infected and end up in the hospital for days instead? Okay. Sounds good to me." Her sarcasm landed with a one-two punch. Colt's lips turned south.

"Fine."

She looked at Georgia. "Both of you to the hospital."

"I'm—"

"Happy to go," Colt offered. "Fair is fair, Georgia Jane."

"Fine."

At the hospital she was treated for a few minor abrasions and to make sure her oxygen levels stayed normal before they released her. Colt entered her curtained room on a crutch. His face was still sooty and streaked. Ash littered his hair, and he reeked of smoke. She no doubt mirrored his appearance and scent.

"Well, aren't we a pair for sore eyes," she said.

"My eyes *are* sore. And I lost a contact, so I can only see clearly out of my left eye. I feel like Popeye, but closing my right is the only way I can actually see anything."

She laughed as he hobbled to the hospital bed and perched beside her, leaning his crutches against the wall.

"At least I always keep a spare pair of contacts in my travel bag. Which happens to be in my truck and not your house. Bright side."

They were alive. Bright side. For now. "I hate that the pain you're experiencing is all because of my big mouth."

With one eye in a consistent wink, he grinned. "While I agree you have a big mouth, this is going down because someone killed Jared Toledo." He ran his fingers through her gritty hair. "I don't know if I've ever been more terrified. I wasn't sure I was going to be able to get you out."

"I was afraid you wouldn't be able to get *you* out."

"Don't worry about me. This is what I signed up for. I'm happy you're safe."

His job.

Safe for now. But no home. She breathed deep. In and out. The worst that could happen is she would live with Susan or Amber awhile or in the back room at the newspaper. She could live with that. Except until the danger passed, she couldn't afford to risk their lives.

"We have to talk about what to do next, Georgia."

"I know." He was going to put her in the motel like he originally wanted.

"First off, you need to bunk with Mae and Poppy at the Magnolia Motel." A dozen years hadn't spared her from knowing him so well.

"They can protect you. Right now, we need to see the Wilcox family. If Jared took the SD card out of his camera, then it might be in his old belongings. If not, then where is it? Did someone else know about it and take it? That brings me to Alice Parker. She might have had motive and she had access to the car while Jared and Chance were inside Rascal's."

Georgia agreed—it was better to work on the case than worry herself sick over Colt. But she couldn't control it. Worry was the name of the game at the moment—and the loser lost their life.

Colt's ankle throbbed and burned as they made their way to Gerald and Karen Wilcox's house. They'd called about an hour ago and asked Amber to be present as well. He inwardly winced at the discomfort, but the upside was his shoulder didn't hurt as much now that the pain was concentrated to his leg. The doc had offered him the good stuff, but he needed all his faculties and had declined it for prescription-strength ibuprofen.

An hour ago, he'd picked it up along with the prescribed antibiotic cream and bandages. The nurse had showed him how to treat the wounds and insisted he keep them clean and freshly wrapped, which he would, but it irritated him. He didn't have time to stop and keep wounds cleaned when a killer was on the loose.

The hours ticked by, making for a long, exhausting day. Reports, interviews about the fire had ensued. A deputy had discovered a plastic gasoline can at the edge of the tree line, and they'd sent it off for prints. No one had been found in the woods, and no other traces of evidence had been obtained.

By nine they'd settled in at the Sunflower Café for breakfast. News had traveled fast, and patrons came in droves to the table, bringing condolences and offers to help keep Georgia safe, as if Colt and his team weren't enough. Maybe he wasn't.

His old man would be the first to say it. Georgia's words about forgiveness being a thing had been quietly rolling around in his chest. Had he forgiven Dad? No. Did he deserve it? No. Talk had made its way through the town and folks were searching out Georgia, but Dad hadn't been among them. Hadn't called to check on him. Nothing. He didn't seem to care if Colt lived or died, so why even offer him an out for his years of cruelty?

The answer puddled in his gut. Because forgiveness wasn't for the offender. It was for the offended.

With God's help he could do anything. All things were possible. But did he want to forgive Dad? Not particularly. Even when he knew deep down it would lift a huge weight from his shoulders. His head battled his heart, reminding him of all the trauma inflicted—the hurtful words and the knocks to the head. They played on repeat, calling out all Colt's failures and defeats.

If he forgave him, Colt might not be controlled by his father's words anymore. That was not the voice he wanted in his head, but it was always there. Taunting. He wanted his heavenly Father's voice. What God thought about him mattered most.

But did God think he was doing a good job?

Shaking out of the battle, he tried to ignore the excruciating burn in his leg. As they pulled into Gerald and Karen's drive, he glanced at Georgia.

This was going to be another tough conversation, but if the SD card was around, they needed all hands on deck to find it.

"Georgia," he said before they walked up to the front porch, "you haven't said much, but I know you're feeling anxious. Afraid. Weak. Even uncertain about the future, but I want you to know that I think you're the bravest woman I've ever known. Your house is in a heap of ashes, and here you are fighting for others and for truth, which kinda sounds comic-book heroic as I hear it coming from my mouth, but it doesn't make it less true."

Georgia paused on the first step of the porch. "I feel like I'm hanging on by a thread. I like to believe that thread is Jesus's strength, or it's going to snap and I'll free fall forever."

They didn't have time to talk this out at the moment, but they would later. "Jesus won't let you fall...and neither will I. Please don't blame yourself for my getting hurt. I'd do it again, you know. Run into a burning building or take a bullet. You need to know that."

She didn't seem to find any solace in those words.

"No," she murmured, "I don't need to know that."

"What do—"

Gerald opened the front door. "Come in, you two. Mercy." He studied Colt's crutches and bandaged foot along with the few abrasions on Georgia's forehead and hands. "Y'all look like you should, I guess. I'm so sorry to hear about your house, Georgia."

He welcomed them into the kitchen, where Amber and Karen sat at the farm table with steaming cups of tea, but the hint of coffee reached Colt's nose. Karen offered them each a choice of drink. Colt accepted coffee, and Georgia declined anything. He'd read anxiety cut appetites; she'd picked at her breakfast.

"Cut to the chase, Colt," Gerald said after everyone was seated.

"All right." He relayed the new developments in the case tying Chance and Scott Hazer to Jared through the pictures at the Magnolia Motel and their meeting at Rascal's. "Which brings me to Alice Parker."

"Alice?" Karen asked. "Why Alice?"

Colt explained Chance's story and that Alice hadn't mentioned seeing Jared that night in her statement. "Why wouldn't she come forward with that pertinent information?"

"Maybe she forgot?" Gerald offered weakly. "She worked from eight to five, five days a week, for me and Friday and Saturday nights at Rascal's. To say she was tired is an understatement. I can't see her purposely withholding information. Why?"

Karen set her teacup on the saucer with shaky fingers. "Alice is a good person and a friend. She must have a good reason. It did somehow slip her mind or Chance Leeway is lying."

Possibly. "We'll know more after we speak with her. But first we have a favor to ask of y'all."

"Anything," Gerald said and reached for Karen's hand.

"We need to go through Jared's things that you might have boxed up." He explained that the SD card was missing. "We need to see those photos. See who Scott was dealing drugs to. Could it have been Alice?"

Gerald and Karen both laughed. "Hardly," Gerald said. "I'd know if one of my office employees was on drugs. Alice was not a druggie."

"What about her son?" Georgia asked. "Wade?"

Gerald's eyes squinted. "I don't think so, but I didn't see him often. He lives in Florida now. Has since he got married."

They needed to call him. He might not tell the truth, but if he had been a teenager who dabbled in pot and then straightened up as he matured, he might be willing to come clean.

"Amber, he would have been in your grade. What do you think?" She sat ramrod straight, face pale and eyes wide. Did she know something she wasn't divulging? That was Colt's gut reaction the first time they'd spoken. But this was her brother. She should want to cooperate.

"I didn't know him well. I never heard any rumors about him using."

But? She was holding back, fidgeting in her chair.

"Can we poke around in anything left of Jared's?" Georgia asked. "It's a long shot, but we might find something."

Karen stood. "Of course. All of his things are in boxes and labeled in the attic. I didn't let go of anything except his clothing to a boys' home. I don't remember finding any little SD cards, though."

If he'd hidden it, she may not have. Could be in a book, a baseball glove…anywhere. It might be a lost cause, but they had to try.

They followed Karen upstairs into the attic. Not too hot for fall. They could have been doing this during the summer months and melted. "I'll help," Karen offered.

"Me too," Gerald said. "More hands, the faster the work."

Amber said nothing, only crept off in the corner.

They combed through boxes for over an hour, reminiscing through laughter and tears, sharing Jared stories as articles that belonged to him ignited memories.

Colt's cell phone rang and drew him from his deep thoughts. He answered.

"Hey, Colt. It's Marcy from the Jackson lab. I got a hit on that print. Sorry it took so long."

"You did?" Hope bloomed in his chest, and he covered the receiver and spoke to Georgia. "Marcy at the Mississippi forensics lab. Prints on Jared's watch popped."

Everyone went on full alert. This could be a huge break.

"Who does it belong to?" he asked Marcy.

"An Alice Parker. Familiar?"

His gut roiled. "Yeah. Thanks."

"Well?" Georgia asked and Karen, Gerald and Amber took a collective step forward.

He shouldn't say it to the family. Her fingerprint didn't prove her guilt. But given she'd worked at Rascal's and Gerald and Karen were adamant she had nothing to do with drugs or Jared… "Alice Parker."

Karen clamped her hand over her mouth, and Gerald stood stupefied, the blood leaching from his cheeks. Amber gasped.

"I don't understand," Karen said in a wobbly voice.

"There must be an explanation," Gerald demanded.

This wasn't a road Colt wanted to travel down, but all avenues needed driven. Jared had been his best friend, full of faith, but he was a teenage boy and Alice Parker had been a looker fifteen years ago. "Could there have been a relationship that would explain her prints on his watch? They'd have to have been fresh, I would imagine. Maybe that night…she was at Rascal's before he died."

Gerald's color returned, bloodred. Colt had crossed

a line but it unfortunately needed exploring. "If you are suggesting that my son had an illicit affair with Alice, then you didn't know him at all."

"I'm sorry, but I have to cover every angle, even the ugly ones, Gerald. I guess she can explain herself. But we have a direct link between them. We'll be looking good and hard." He slid his gaze to Amber, who remained silent. "Now's the time to tell what needs told if there is anything."

When no one spoke, he motioned Georgia to follow him down the attic stairs, each step reminding him of the searing wound from the fire. Colt didn't expect anyone to follow him out or wish him well. He'd just cast a stone at their son.

As they reached his truck, Georgia sighed. "You don't think Alice Parker and Jared…"

"No. But he was there in the summers. Holiday breaks. Occasional weekdays. Who knows? But bases weren't covered fifteen years ago and the case went cold. I can't afford not to cover them now."

She laid her purse on the floorboard. "I understand. It could be as simple as she reached out and grabbed him because he forgot his jacket. Chance said he laid it on the chair and searched it when Jared went to the restroom."

"Maybe." He started the engine. "If Alice had come forward about seeing Jared the night he died, then a simple answer like that would be believable. But she didn't."

"If she's linked at all to Chance or his father, she might have been too afraid to talk. Reggie Leeway is a powerful man." Georgia situated Colt's crutches so they wouldn't fall on her. "You need to rest that leg at some point."

No time. They were close. He called his team as he backed out of the drive. "Hey, I got news."

"Us too," Poppy said. They were on speakerphone as well. "Go first."

He laid out the new info and where they were headed. "What do you have?"

Rhett spoke up. "I got in touch with Tyler Burgess's mom, and she admitted that Harry Benard approached her about using the address, but it was Reggie Leeway who called her after Georgia's attack and told her to respond with 'no comment' if she was questioned by anyone. He said she'd be rewarded monetarily. But she said it wasn't worth it."

"Harry's dead. That dog won't hunt."

"True. That's not all, though. We got a call earlier from Carter Wagoner, one of athletes who used the address the year the land was purchased. He said that his dad was out of a job and they were going to lose their house, but then they didn't. Next thing Carter knows, he's transferring to Courage High and his dad told him it was for the best and not to ask questions. Guess where the house loan went through?"

"Terry Helms's bank."

"And guess what that did?" Poppy asked.

"Got you a warrant for bank records regarding the students' families who used 4214 Pine Road."

"Well, you took all the fun out of that," she huffed.

Rhett cleared his throat, and Colt could imagine him rolling his eyes at Poppy's dramatics. "We did. With a different judge. We're on our way there now. If he was falsifying information, we'll find it. Anything at all to do with 4214 Pine Road is within our scope."

"Keep me posted." He hung up.

Georgia grinned. "Terry is involved. And Coach Flanigan—probably Sunny Wilkerson. One of them has been attacking me and probably killed Dandy—but what about Jared?"

"I don't know. It doesn't seem connected to the athletic department. What if Jared accepted the offer to play for Ole Magnolia without telling his parents? He was eighteen. Then changed his mind and was going to tell the coach the night he died that he was reneging on the deal so he could play for State instead. Maybe the phone call stopped him short. Or maybe he did tell Coach and he conveniently left that part out. Coach could have asked him to meet him later—after the workout. Then killed him. Or he could have told Terry or Sunny, and one of them killed him."

"Why kill him and bring him back to the training room?"

"Throw the scent off him. Because it makes no sense. But more likely he was moved because the killer didn't want the location of his murder discovered. It would reveal the killer's identity."

They parked along the curb near the courthouse and walked inside. After going through security, they entered the clerk's office. Alice Parker might have aged fifteen years, but she didn't look a day over forty-five or-six. Her hair hung at shoulder length, dark and wavy, and her sharp green eyes matched her business suit. She did a double take. "Colt McCoy!" Then she noticed his crutches, and a mother's concern radiated in her tone and facial expression. "Honey, what on earth happened to you?"

"You hear about Georgia's house?"

"Yes. I heard after lunch. I'm sorry, hon. That's awful.

Where are you staying? I'm gonna bring you a pie." Yes, because pie would help, but in crises that's what folks did. Bring food.

"Thank you. I'm staying at the Magnolia Motel with the cold case unit."

A flash of disapproval flared in her eyes.

"I'm gonna cut to the chase," Colt said. "We ran old evidence, and this time we got a hit on prints from Jared's watch. They're yours."

ELEVEN

"Well, that went about as expected," Georgia said through a frustrated huff as Colt pulled out onto the main highway. Alice had been appalled that they would even think to implicate her in a murder. She'd loved Jared like her own son and would never have harmed him.

"Did you believe her when she said she didn't remember Jared and Chance being in Rascal's that night?" Georgia asked.

"Not particularly. Chance was confident she'd back him up. She seemed well versed, but her eyes held unease and quite frankly some hidden truth. I'd like to get my hands on that SD card. Without it I don't know what comes next."

And he was leaving in a few weeks. Leaving her alone with his unit was well and good; she trusted them. But they weren't Colt. That line of thinking was why it was best for him to go and the sooner the better. She already lay awake at night fretting about the next day and what might happen to him.

Georgia's phone rang. "It's Amber. I'm gonna put her on speaker." She hit the green button and answered. "Hey, Amber, what's up?"

"Hey. I need to talk to you. I wanted to do it at the house, but I couldn't bring myself to." Her voice was nasally, as if she'd been crying. "I have to come in to work. Can you meet me at the stables?"

"Yes, of course. What's this about?"

She sniffed. "I'm sorry. I have the SD card."

Georgia and Colt shared a shocked exchange with one another. "Did you find it?"

"No. I had it. I apologize for putting y'all through all that worthless searching. I was…I was struggling, but I got to do what's right."

"We're on our way," Georgia said and hung up. Colt made a U-turn on the highway and headed to the south end of town. Milford's Stables was on the left before one crossed into Craw County. Amber had worked here since she was sixteen. Now, she managed them.

"Why would Amber have the SD card?" Colt's brow knit as he gripped the wheel and concentrated on the road. "Do you think this was part of their fighting? If Jared knew she'd taken it somehow…"

Georgia tossed her hands up. "We keep running into more questions than answers. I have no idea what to believe at this point. But if Amber has the SD card, then Alice didn't take it. And how would Alice even know about it?"

"Scott knew about it. If Alice's son, Wade, was in the photos with him, Jared could have approached him in an effort to turn Wade from his ways. He was like that. Or Scott told Wade and he told his mom out of fear?"

Alice's prints on the watch may have been about the SD card and her son. "Or Jared approached Wade and threatened to tell Alice if he didn't quit dabbling in drugs, or he did tell Alice in an attempt to help him before it got out of hand."

"That makes Wade Parker a suspect, and he lives in Florida. We need to send someone out there to talk to him."

The road stretched into miles of pastureland where cattle grazed and horses roamed, eating grass and moseying, not a single worry in the world. Must be nice.

Colt turned on the road that led to the stables. He parked next to Amber's red Jeep in front of the office. The secretary there told them Amber was in the stables. They entered, the smells of hay and manure whacking Georgia in the face.

Amber stood, petting a horse's mane.

"Hey," Georgia said.

Amber wiped her wet lashes. "I'm sorry for everything."

"We need the truth, Amber."

She inhaled deeply. "I was scared to tell my parents that I'd been seeing Scott. I knew he and Jared had gotten into it. Scott told me that Jared had followed him one night and taken pictures of him at the motel while he was dealing drugs. He said Jared threatened to take them to the police if he didn't stop hanging around me."

"So you took the card to protect Scott?"

"Scott promised to get out of the business. Said he hated it but was forced by someone older in his family. I picked up every word he put down."

Naive girls.

"I sneaked into Jared's car before he left to go work out at the school and stole the card. I was prepared to fight about it when he discovered it missing, but he...he died. I believed this person Scott had alluded to—who turned out to be fictitious—killed Jared over the photos and it was all my fault."

Amber slumped to her knees and held her face in her hands. "He's dead because of what I did."

Amber believed Scott killed Jared. Georgia grappled with being angry with Amber for withholding important information all these years and feeling compassion for an old friend who had carried the guilt of her brother's death.

Georgia knelt beside her. "You told the truth now. You have the card. And you don't know for sure that Scott killed Jared." Why would he if he knew Chance was stealing the incriminating evidence that would clear him? Unless he wasn't as dumb as Chance suspected and knew the real card was missing. He let Chance believe it was over so he wouldn't suspect him of killing Jared.

"Have you looked at what's on the SD card?" Colt asked.

Amber shook her head. "I didn't want to see it. At first for fear Scott's boss might find me and kill me, too. That's why I never told Scott I had it. I was too afraid to give it to the police. Over the years, I've forgotten about it as I've moved on. But every anniversary I remember and wonder what would have happened if I'd been brave enough to do the right thing."

She'd been a seventeen-year-old girl. Teenagers make dumb decisions. Amber stood and handed Colt the SD card. "I hope whoever is on there is found and the truth comes out. I'm so sorry."

Colt patted her shoulder and pocketed the SD card.

The secretary poked her head inside and hollered, "Hey, I'm running out. It's just you, Amber. I turned the voice mail on to catch any calls. Be back in an hour."

Amber nodded and waved. When she left, Amber turned to Colt. "Do you think Scott killed Jared?"

"Maybe. I need to see what's on here first and talk to him again. Things are surfacing."

"What did Alice say?"

"I can't divulge detailed information, but she claims innocence." Colt sneezed. "Hay." He shrugged. "Is there anything else I need to know? Now really is the time to air it all out."

"That's it. I promise."

Georgia wanted to believe her but she'd lied before. "We'll be in touch."

She followed Colt to the truck. "You thinking what I'm thinking?" Georgia asked.

"That we need a digital camera or a computer that will accept the SD card?"

"Yeah."

Colt eased down the long drive to the main road. He relayed his thoughts, which matched what she was thinking about Scott being smarter than he looked. "But wouldn't Scott have realized that if the card was missing that Amber—who knew about it—would have it? Why not approach her?"

"No need. He was in no danger from her."

Scott looked like the killer. But they still had Alice's unexplained prints on Jared's watch, which indicated she'd grabbed him by the wrist or held it on at least one finger, as if handing it back to him. Georgia tended to believe she'd grabbed him—as if to wait, or to keep him from leaving.

But why?

None of this led to the illegal recruiting ring.

Colt turned into a sharp curve on the hill, and Georgia heard his foot pumping the brakes. "What—Georgia, we have no brakes!" Colt leaned into the turn, but they were picking up speed. Georgia's pulse spiked, and she clutched the door and braced herself.

Colt tried to turn the wheel, but it was locked in place. "Power steering is gone! I have no control, Georgia. None!" He voiced a prayer to God for help, and then the truck jumped the edge of the curve and went airborne, over a small embankment before crashing into horse fencing and landing with a deafening thud that rattled every bone in Georgia's body.

The world tilted.

She blinked and caught Colt in her periphery, his head against the steering wheel, blood trickling down the side of his face. The windshield had been spiderwebbed after having it fixed yesterday morning. She tried to open the door.

Jammed.

"Colt," she whispered through a hoarse throat. "Colt." She fought to produce more sound. Had someone messed with their brakes and steering wheel? When? Must have been at the stables. They'd been followed.

Which meant the killer wasn't far behind. He'd be expecting an accident—their death. If he'd been watching, had he seen Amber hand them the SD card? Was she in danger, too?

Her faculties were fuzzy, but she had enough of them to know they couldn't stay here. Their saving grace was they'd gone over the hilly curve and couldn't be seen from the road—but whoever followed them might know. Time wasn't on their side.

Everything ached, and it was excruciating to even

shift in the seat. She unbuckled and reached for Colt. What if he was dead? No. He couldn't be.

God, Your grace is sufficient and You are strong when I am weak. I don't know if I've ever been weaker, so I need Your strength. Help me, help us.

She touched Colt's shoulder, and it slumped. This could not be happening. Her worst fears coming to reality. "Colt?" She forced her body to move and guided her shaky fingers to Colt's neck, checking for a pulse. She found one!

"Okay. I can work with that," she muttered aloud and glanced up the hill. She couldn't carry Colt up it, and hitchhiking was out. They'd give their position away. Maybe the culprit behind this hadn't seen the wreck and he was up on the road searching. That gave her a few extra moments to rouse Colt from unconsciousness.

"Come on, Colton." Jostling him too much might further injure him if he was severely hurt. And if he was, then how on earth was she going to manage getting him to safety? With her own body protesting and her ears ringing, she leaned into him, her lips on his scruffy cheek as she murmured into his ear, "Colt, I need you to wake up." She squeezed her eyes closed, afraid he might not make it out and she might not, either. "Wake up. You can't die on me. I won't let you. Do not let my worst fear become reality."

A big engine revved nearby. Probably a truck. Adrenaline kicked in a second time. *God, help me, because I have no choice.*

Georgia crawled into the back seat of the truck and pulled the door handle. It opened. She stumbled out and hobbled on weak legs to the driver's-side door. She yanked it open and carefully but quickly leaned Colt back so she could reach across him and undo his seat belt. He had a pretty sick gash on his forehead. She winced but kept moving.

She was no skinny minnie or weakling, but Colt was a big guy and solid muscle. He was a dead man if she didn't help him. Pulling him toward her, his limp body hung over her shoulder, the weight of him pressing her down until she lost her footing but regained it.

The other truck's engine idled, as if someone was scouring the roadside for their vehicle.

Heart and mind racing, she prayed and backed up until his entire body was slung over her, his feet dragging on the ground, but she had most of him relying on her. She ignored the fire in her shoulders, back and legs and began walking backward away from the SUV toward the small dip under the hill. If the killer came down, he'd see an empty truck, but if he looked hard enough, he'd find them. She spotted Colt's gun on his hip. With shaking hands, she drew it and switched off the safety.

Footfalls on debris above sounded.

He was coming.

"Mr. McCoy," an unfamiliar feminine voice said. Colt cracked open his eyes, and a young woman with auburn hair smiled. "You gave us all a scare." Nurse. She was in scrubs.

His head felt like it'd been hit with a two-by-four, and his entire body ached. The prior events registered. Brake lines and power steering fluid released...they'd crashed.

Georgia!

Colt bolted upright, instantly regretting it but unable to care. "Where's Georgia?" he hollered, panic gripping him by the throat.

"I'm here. Right here." Georgia stood and took his hand.

Rhett, Poppy and Mae were leaning against the wall by the door to the hospital room. Rhett edged to the end of his bed. "Miss Armchair Detective here saved your bacon today."

Poppy snickered.

Georgia smiled, but the right side of her face was bruised and her wrist was wrapped. The light in her eyes didn't shine quite so brightly.

"What happened?"

"You hit your head pretty hard and were knocked unconscious. Minor concussion," Georgia said. She brushed hair from his forehead. "Got a few stitches from hitting your head on the steering wheel. The airbag didn't deploy."

"Forensics took the truck. Brake lines were cut and the powering steering fluid holder had been punctured. Probably already figured that when you couldn't stop or turn." Poppy huffed. "We're gonna get this guy."

"He almost got you," Mae said and nodded her chin toward Georgia. "But she managed to drag and carry your big self out of the vehicle and to a little nook in the hill. When the attacker started down the slope, she fired your gun, and I guess he didn't want to risk a shootout with a trained agent. Must have thought it was you shooting. He took off, but she says the truck was a big engine. Big roar."

Colt stared at Georgia. "You…you carried me?"

"I had a pretty big shot of adrenaline running through me. I couldn't leave you there. He would have seen you and…" Her eyes filled with moisture.

"Can we have a few moments?"

The team gave him knowing grins and left the room.

"Georgia, I can't begin to thank you enough and I'm... I'm shocked. You carried *me*."

She perched on the hospital bed next to him, her hand on his. "He definitely followed us. I can't say for sure if he knew we had the SD card or not."

"I don't know how he could. Unless it was Chance, Alice or Scott."

"Or Reggie Leeway. He's connected to everyone. Coaches. His son. Scott. I've had some time to think while you were in here."

This woman was amazing. Riddled with anxiety or not, she had singlehandedly saved him. She was strong and brave. He laced his hand with hers and drew her toward him. All he could think about was the kiss they hadn't talked about. He'd chalked it up to a mistake. But it wasn't. In fact, it was all he wanted to do in this moment.

This wild woman had rescued him, used her brain and shot a round off to save them.

He wasn't sure what the future held, but right now he wanted it to hold him and Georgia. "I—I know we haven't talked about that kiss, Georgia. But I want to. And to be honest, I want to kiss you again." They could figure out the logistics, couldn't they? "You told me you weren't sure if you loved me back then, but that was a lie. What about relationships? Was that a lie, too? Why did we really end?" There had to be a good reason, one they could work through.

Georgia sighed and lifted herself off the hospital bed. "I can't." She hesitated as if fighting the words about to come from her lips.

Rejection.

He'd put himself out there, and he was going to get it

again. Even with all the effort he'd put into protecting her, showing he was a worthy man—he'd failed. What was it about him that was so easy to throw away?

Georgia closed her eyes and sniffed, then opened her eyes but refused to look at him. "You're right. You deserve to know the truth. I've always wanted to get married."

"You lied about that, too. Why?"

Georgia blinked, and tears washed down her cheeks. "I was sick all the time. Nagging you. I was tired of feeling the fear, and the only way I knew to get any peace was to end things. Because if I ended it then I'd stop loving you, and if I stopped loving you I wouldn't worry myself into a daily frenzy over you."

Colt didn't understand. That made no sense. She'd loved him. He'd loved her.

"Colt... I didn't know what was going on with me then. I do now. I avoid my triggers."

"But I told you I'd never do anything to trigger your anxiety, Georgia Jane. All you have to do is tell me what they are and I'll avoid them, too." *Please don't reject me again.* He wasn't sure he'd recover from another one. Not from her. Not when he'd let his heart get out of check. Let his guard down.

Grief robbed the light in her eyes and sagged her mouth. "Oh, Colt. I wish it were that simple."

"Why isn't it?"

"Because you *are* the trigger. People I love die, and because of that, I worry about them incessantly until I'm physically too sick to function. I have acquaintances and colleagues. I don't date. Amber and Susan are probably the closest things to a friend, but we don't hang out or go to dinner. I can't afford to love somebody. I can't compromise my mental and physical health to love you. Even if I want to."

"Do you? Want to?" He wasn't sure which answer would kill him the most. If she did want to and wouldn't or if she didn't want to at all.

"I think that kiss tells the tale, don't you?"

He clenched his jaw to hold in the emotion. "I think you owe me the words from your own lips." If he forced her to admit she wanted to be with him, then maybe she would change her mind. There had to be a way. More medicines. Something. Anything.

Georgia touched his cheek. "You're right. Yes, I want to. I kissed you because I feel something for you and I entertained the idea, and then you were shot and burned and now this. And it's not only this isolated event. When the killer is caught, it won't be over. Because it's what you do. You said it. You signed up for this. Taking bullets and running into raging infernos and risking being in a killer's grip every single day."

Reality sank in like a millstone around his neck and invisible hands shoving him into the ocean deep.

"If I threw up every Friday over football, imagine what it would do to me every single day watching you strap on your gun and leave the house. Colt, trust me. You don't want to commit yourself to this. You'll regret it and resent me. And I'd hate myself. I already do."

"But you made it through the gunshots—granted, with some panic, but I helped you. And then we made it through the house fire. You put my fire out. You carried me from a vehicle."

"I did. What choice did I have? But what you can't see isn't happening on the outside. I know I seem fine. I look super chill most of the time, but since the fire… I've been a wreck. I've had to call my therapist three times. Not to mention I was with you in these circumstances. What happens when you have to travel and I can't be right there to watch over you like you watch over me?"

"I have a team."

"I know. You had a team in football, too."

There was no point arguing. She'd resolved to go her entire life alone. While she wasn't rejecting him over him personally, it still felt like a hot blade in his gut. His job kept them apart, but even if he offered up his job on the altar of sacrifice—she'd still turn him down. And he'd worked hard and long for his position. Even if he said he'd stay in Mississippi, she'd decline. It didn't matter.

"I'm sorry. The last thing I ever wanted was to hurt you." She leaned in and tenderly kissed his cheek. "Get some rest. I'll be with the team."

She left him speechless and feeling like he'd never been rescued from that burning quilt at all. His heart was in pieces all over again. He'd promised himself he'd never let it crumble over her—over anyone—again, but here he was.

He was her trigger. Not something he might do, but him. Hope for them was dead in the water.

And he was left alone. Not even his own father had shown up. But Colt hadn't reached out to him, either. Maybe it was the concussion. Maybe it was the overwhelming loneliness he felt at the moment or the little boy who had only wanted his father's approval and love—the little boy who had done everything in his power to make him proud. The junior high boy who had cleaned and cooked and never asked for anything. The high school boy who got clobbered at football practices and games to make his father proud.

Or it could be a combination of everything, but he picked up his phone to reach out with the last sliver of hope that Dad would give a flying flip that his only son had almost died.

He hit the button, and it rang once, twice, three times.

"Hello," his dad said with that deep, raspy, impatient tone.

"Hey, Dad, it's Colt."

He grunted. "Heard you was in town investigating that Toledo kid's case."

"I am." His stomach was in a million knots. "Taken a beatin' but I think we're getting somewhere. I'm…I'm actually in the hospital." Would he come?

"I heard you got hurt. Got burned in that girl's house fire. Still trying to be her hero?" His laugh was cold and hard. "You never gonna listen, are you, boy? That girl don't want you. No matter how many burning homes you run into or bullets you take."

"I know," he whispered. *Believe me, I know.* "Doesn't mean I won't keep trying to save her." Colt wiped the tear leaking from his eye. "I just—" His voice cracked, and he balled his fist. "I wanted you to know that even though I've been in some accidents, I'm okay." He should have known better than to call. But a deep pressing in his bones wouldn't let up. Even now. Even in this moment, he should forgive.

"I never thought you'd be good at that job. Gonna end up dead before you're forty."

Colt swallowed the disappointment and crushing blow. He was never going to make his earthly father happy. Not one day on this planet.

But he could make his heavenly Father proud and pleased. "Well…I guess we'll see."

"I gotta go. Got a car I'm working on. Said I'd have it done by this evening."

"Right." Because a car was more important than his son in a hospital. "Hey, Dad."

"Yep?"

"I—I forgive you." The words tumbled out and a boulder was lifted from his chest, making some breathing room. All the past. All the pain. Colt chose to release it.

"Well, I didn't ask for it. And don't rightly see why I'd need it."

"I know you don't." Maybe one day he would. Maybe not. Colt wasn't responsible for Dad's choices and actions. Only his own. And his next choice was getting out of this place. He had a job to do, and that was top priority.

He left his room and Georgia came around the corner with a coffee in her hand. "What are you doing up?"

"I have a case to solve."

"Oh." Questions swirled in her eyes. Were they okay? Was he angry? He was too tired to be angry.

"I called my dad."

She gaped. "For real?"

"Apparently forgiveness is a thing."

"How did that go?"

He could actually laugh. "Not like I hoped. But then, nothing about this day has gone like I hoped."

She dropped her head. "I'm so sorry, Colt."

"I know. I understand, Georgia. You gotta do what you gotta do. I'm gonna do what I gotta do, and it is what it is. At least we know where we stand with one another." Not exactly profound words, but truthful. Would he want to press their relationship knowing she would be sick with anxiety every day? No. He didn't want that, and mostly he hated that she was imprisoned by it. That was no way to live. But he wasn't responsible for her choices, either.

Rhett met them as they turned the corner. "Hey, I was coming to give you the news. We got the warrant, and guess what we found in Terry Helms's financials?"

"Proof that Terry had something to do with buying the land on Pine Road?"

Rhett's grin was full of satisfaction. "James Kreger isn't a real person, as we suspected. But we found papers where he secured a loan through the bank—it didn't go through any of the loan officers, but Terry himself. There are statements that the loan is being paid, but we haven't gotten far enough to see if Terry is actually paying on the land—we didn't get the warrant to cover the scope of Terry's personal finances, only information pertaining to the land."

This was excellent information. "Where is Terry now?"

"Station. We asked him to come in, and he obliged. Of course, Poppy threatened to haul him out of the bank in cuffs." His eyes held amusement. "Aren't you supposed to be in a hospital bed? You have a mild concussion on top of other injuries."

"I have too much to do and too little time." They didn't talk much about the move to Atlanta. It was bittersweet. "We need to see what's on this SD card."

Rhett gave him grief over not following the rules. Typical, but in the end, he conceded and Colt and Georgia climbed in the SUV, since his truck was totaled.

Inside the station interview room, Terry Helms sat in the folding chair, his big, meaty hands resting on the table. Colt hobbled in with his crutches, and Georgia followed.

Terry's eyes widened. "What happened to you?"

"I have a feeling you already know." Colt finagled into a seat.

Time to get to the truth.

TWELVE

"I didn't try to kill anyone! Not Jared and not you, Georgia." Terry folded his arms over his massive chest, and protest radiated in his eyes.

"What about Dandy?" Colt asked.

"What about her? I didn't kill her. I'm not a murderer."

"Someone is. We have proof that those boys falsified their addresses using land purchased with a fake loan. One you signed off on. The jig is up."

Georgia pursed her lips.

Okay, that may have sounded a bit like *Scooby-Doo*.

Terry remained silent, but he hadn't asked for a lawyer. Any minute Colt was bound to see Reggie Leeway waltz through the door. "You know what we've already uncovered. Before it's over we'll find more. Help us now. If you didn't kill anyone, then come clean on the rest. You'll more than likely get a slap from the NCAA for your part in illegal recruiting to Ole Magnolia." Of course, he'd lose his job for falsifying documents, and have to face fraud charges for the Pine Road address.

He knew it, too. It showed in the slump of his shoulders and the defeat on his face. "I bought the land through a fake name. Fake address. Handled all the paperwork so no one would be the wiser. Yeah, I did that. I may have helped families get loans that they may not have been able to receive at another bank, but they legit have paid off those loans or are still paying on them. But that's helping them."

"Who's involved? I want it all and maybe it'll go toward helping you. Can't say for sure."

Terry huffed. "We love our town and our team. We did it to help boys who deserved to go pro or at the very least play college ball. We did it to put our town and team on the map in football. We win championships. Nothing wrong with that."

Except it was cheating.

"Who is we?"

Terry massaged the back of his neck. "Me, Duncan, Sunny and Joe Jackson."

So the coach at Ole Magnolia was involved. A nice little thing going. Colt would be sure to give the NCAA a call after this interrogation. Terry's story unfolded the way they'd suspected—they poached players from other districts to come play for them with loan offers, monetary offers as well as sealed deals with Ole Magnolia if they continued to perform in their high school career. It kept the coaches in the spotlight and won them championships and fame, not to mention Coach Flanigan received some kickbacks from the college for bringing them top players—according to Terry. Coach had yet to admit that.

"What about Jared? Did you offer him the deal at Ole Magnolia?"

Terry nodded. "We gave him tickets to a concert he was wanting to attend and about ten grand."

Ten grand! Wow.

"But he died and that was that. Never even asked for the money back. It was a tragedy."

"How kind of you," Georgia stated dryly.

But Jared was going to go play for State. Terry and Coach had no idea he'd changed his mind—or Terry was lying.

"Jared changed his mind. Did you know that?"

"No. None of us knew that, though Duncan suspected. Said Jared had come in and wanted to talk to him—seemed upset and he figured it was a change of heart. Said he'd talk to Gerald and see what was going on, but then we found out Sunday morning that Jared had been murdered."

Colt paused. "Gerald knew Jared had accepted an illegal offer to play ball?" He and Karen had both denied those allegations. All these years.

"Of course."

Gerald knew. Karen knew. They must have hidden that to protect Jared and their reputations. They wouldn't have been arrested for it. Might have to give back the money if the NCAA requested them to. If they hadn't hidden it, then investigators could have gone down a recruiting angle avenue long ago. Colt made a note to call them on it and find out why they felt the need to keep it concealed.

"Talk to me about Georgia's attacks, Dandy Martin's and Harry Benard's murders. If you did it, or if you're an accomplice, I can talk to the DA and he might be willing to go easy on you. If you cooperate."

Terry looked at Georgia, and his hands went up in surrender. "I never killed or hurt anyone. I admit I heard about your podcast from a loan officer at my bank—Tricia Candor. Ask her. She told me, and I listened to it and told Duncan. I suspected it was about Jared, but Duncan knew it was, and he knew it was you, Georgia. Said you mentioned something about truth rising in an ocean or something. Said you said the exact same thing to him when you were questioning people about Jared's death in high school. We hoped it wouldn't amount to anything, and then you got attacked and we figured…"

Figured someone else would take care of it and they could sit pretty. Vultures.

"I said, 'My mama used to tell me that time will lift the truth to the surface and it'll bob in the water of lies for all to see.' Like it is right now."

But who else knew it was Georgia? Anyone who knew that she used that phrase. Or Duncan had attacked Georgia and kept it from Terry. Or Terry was flat-out lying.

"Did Dandy come around with questions?" Colt asked.

"She did. Came asking Duncan and me questions about Pine Road. We talked about what to do and if bribing her might work, but then she died in a carjacking."

"Convenient," Georgia spewed. "It's all too convenient."

"What about Harry Benard? Miss Thompson and Miss Burgess both said he came to them about playing for the Cougars. Why is he dead?"

"How would I know? Harry never liked the recruiting. Felt it was unfair. We were glad to see him go, but he knew not to say a word because he'd caved and done the dirty work with the Burgess and Thompson boys. Needed the money." Harry had taken money. Did the deed. Felt bad and when the Tigers coaching position opened up, he transferred.

"And he conveniently died before we could question him. Again, *I'm* saying it." Georgia folded her arms over her chest, fire in her eyes. "Come clean, Terry. This is ridiculous."

"I am coming clean. I'm going to lose my bank position by admitting the truth about Pine Road."

"No," Colt said. "We busted you out on that. Sit tight." He signaled Georgia to follow him out, and the team rallied. "With the fraud charges, we have enough to get a warrant to search his home for guns and knives."

"On it," Poppy said and disappeared.

"We also have enough to bring in Duncan Flanigan."

Rhett nodded. "Already took the liberty of asking him to come in and answer a few questions about Harry Benard—whom we suspect of recruiting athletes. He was more than happy to throw Benard under the bus."

Little did he know. "Good. We need to see what's on this SD card, figure out why Alice had her prints on Jared's watch and if she's involved. Mae, can you find a camera or a computer to fit this brand of SD card?" He showed it to her, and she took a picture of it.

"On it."

Poppy rounded the corner. "Coach Duncan Flanigan is here."

Inside the interview room, Coach met Colt's eyes with smugness. This guy actually believed he was getting off scot-free and Harry Benard was going to go down for it all. "Whatever I can do to help you in regards to Harry, let me know."

"We'll get to Harry. Let's start with your attack on Georgia after Terry Helms informed you of her podcast. You recognized her truth-and-lies phrase. Told Terry you knew it was her."

"All true, except I didn't attack her."

"No? Okay." He was going to stick to his guns. For

now. "We know about Pine Road. We had parents confirm. Former athletes."

Coach's bravado faltered, but he held his resolve.

"See, Terry is in a room across the hall, and he's already given it up." He laid it all out, letting it sink in. Coach balled a fist, and a vein bulged in his neck. "It won't be long before those boys have to go back to their right district." Time to hit him where it would hurt most. "And your career as a cheater—it's over."

"I didn't cheat." He leaned forward, obviously hating that label. "I recruited good players. I gave them an education and a shot at the NFL. I put this town on the map. It'd be nothing without me." His pride was almost tangible.

"You are a cheater and liar, and you don't deserve a single title. You didn't grow boys into the best—you stole the best to make yourself look good."

A vein popped in Coach's forehead as his face turned murderous. His pride wouldn't let him keep silent. Colt had seen it one too many times.

Georgia intervened. "What will the town think when they find out that their state championships were built on everything false—that some of the best players had to be brought in under the table?"

"You shut your mouth, girlie!" Coach slammed his hands on the table. "I'll tell you what I told Dandy Martin. If you'd keep your mouth shut, things would keep going well. You and she are going to wreck these boys' dreams. But she wouldn't listen, either."

Colt jumped in. "And you had to shut Dandy up like you tried to shut up Georgia."

"You're right I did!" He blurted his admission of guilt without even realizing it, like a play right out of Jack

Nicholson's book in *A Few Good Men*. But Colt wasn't shocked at his admission. He'd been expecting it.

Coach went on ranting. "People like you jump in and stick your noses where they don't belong. No one was hurting you."

"Until you hurt me!"

Suddenly, the fact he'd admitted guilt hit him and he sank in his chair. Defeated. Outed.

"You killed Dandy for poking around. Thought it was all over. But then Georgia got her notes and started connecting dots and went live on her podcast. She was going to find you, and you attacked her, hoping to shut her up permanently, but I showed up. Even that didn't stop you. Did you bribe Jared? It's over, Duncan. It's time to tell the whole truth."

Duncan licked his bottom lip, knowing the home team was up too many points for him to recover and win the game.

"Terry and I did offer Jared incentive. He took the money and the concert tickets. We signed the agreement, and it was a done deal."

"Who is we?"

"Me, Terry as a witness and Joe." The Ole Magnolia coach. "I had a feeling he was regretting the decision that night he came to me. But he got that call and said never mind—that part is all true. I do regret leaving that night. I do wish I knew more. I didn't kill Jared Toledo."

"But you did kill Dandy Martin, and you attempted to kill Georgia."

"Look me in the eye and admit it, Duncan," Georgia demanded.

He gradually made eye contact. "You should have

kept your mouth shut and stuck to the Podunk crimes that happen around here."

No apology. He didn't believe he was wrong. This town had made him a king, and he believed it. But it was over now. Except he hadn't admitted to killing Jared. And Colt tended to believe him. "What about Harry Benard?"

"Harry never liked the idea of what we were doing. But he didn't seem to mind the wins. We pressed him to talk to the Burgess and Thompson families. If we could get some dirt on him, he'd keep everything under wraps. He needed money for his sister's medical bills. We offered him a onetime deal, and he took it. But he left. Big deal. We knew he'd never talk. Until things got heated and y'all showed up. When Leeway called to cancel a meeting I'd arranged—to put some additional pressure on him—I couldn't be sure what he was up to. I went over there, saw he really was at home and did what had to be done."

"And Terry? Did he help you?"

"No. He helped recruit and offer incentives as well as supply the address. Never hurt anyone." At least the coach wasn't going to take Terry down with him on murder charges or conspiracy to commit murder.

"I think we've heard enough." Colt and Georgia left the room.

Outside in the hall, he didn't know what to do. Hug her? That seemed out of the question. Instead, he sighed. "You're out of danger, at least, and it's almost over."

She would remain and put the charred pieces of her life back together, and he was going to move on to Atlanta. There was nothing left for him here. Not when he was her trigger, and law enforcement was who he was.

She wrapped her arms around herself as if she wasn't sure what gesture to make, either. "I can hardly believe it. You did a really good job, Colt. Thank you." Her phone rang. "It's the vet." She answered and listened a few moments. "No. No need for them to stay a few more days. I'll be there. Thanks." She ended the call and pocketed her phone. "Picking up the dogs." She chewed her bottom lip. "I know you have a lot to wrap up here. Susan is actually at the station bringing her brother dinner, so I'll bum a ride from her. It'll be great having my boys back again."

And they didn't have to be in a car again with the weirdness. "I have paperwork."

He needed Duncan to write out a statement about the illegal recruiting ring and Dandy's and Harry's murders, as well as the attacks on Georgia, her dogs and Colt. He'd also need a statement from Terry Helms, and he wanted to speak to Sunny Wilkerson again. They were waiting to hear from Wade Parker in Florida, and Alice would need more questioning. One of them would hopefully cop to killing Jared. Then he could move on.

"Well…again…thank you for being here and sticking it out. And I wish you well in Atlanta, if I don't see you again." Her lip quivered, but she sucked it between her teeth and put on a brave face. "Have you got a place there already?"

"No. I'll start that this upcoming week. What about you? Where will you stay? What are you going to do?" As of now she was homeless.

"I have insurance. I'll probably end up rebuilding, but for now I'm going to see if Amber will let me and the dogs stay with her. Susan's apartment doesn't allow pets. That's about all I know, which isn't much, but it's enough, I guess."

Did he stick out his hand for a shake or...? He went with his gut and gave her a friendly hug. Kept it short. "I guess this is technically goodbye."

She held his gaze, then bit her bottom lip and dipped her chin once in a nod. "I wish—"

"Let's not do that," he murmured. He didn't want her wishes. "Take care of yourself, Georgia Jane. I'll be listening to your podcasts."

She laughed. "I may hang up my podcast hat for a while."

"Probably be safer, and you need a better name." He found he could actually grin. "I can't just shoot over here from Atlanta if you get in trouble again."

"I suppose not. But I'm not out until Jared's killer is caught."

"I expected as much, but we found your attacker and that gives me a measure of peace."

"Me too." She shifted her feet and glanced down the hall. "I need to find Susan."

He watched her walk away from him.

Once again.

He didn't think it could hurt worse than the first time. But it did.

Georgia loved on her babies, but it didn't mend her broken heart. Didn't change the fact she couldn't be with the only man she'd ever loved. Walking away from him was the hardest thing she'd ever done—and she'd hauled him from a truck and carried him to a dip in a hill. She'd watched him get shot and put out a fiery quilt on his leg. But saying goodbye—knowing he wanted her but knowing she couldn't walk that road—was the worst thing she'd ever done in her life. If she wasn't so riddled with anxiety...if...if...if...

"Wow," Susan said, "those pups are happy to see you."

"I missed them. Thanks for giving me a ride to the vet and to Amber's."

"Girl, please. I'm happy to do it."

"I'm glad it's over. These few days have been a living nightmare."

"But you made it, and you have a great story to tell. I can't believe Coach Flanigan tried to kill you. I can't believe he killed Dandy." Tears pooled in her eyes. "I would have never guessed it. Do you think he'll end up admitting to Jared's death? It stinks that no one is copping to that. Why? Why lie about that after admitting he murdered two people and tried to kill you?"

"I don't know. They still have Alice's prints on Jared's watch and an SD card to look at. That might shed some light on who killed him if no one fesses up. But Colt feels like the light is at the end of the tunnel, and my attacker has been caught, so I'm free to move on."

Susan turned on Oleander Drive. "Will it be with him? He's only forty minutes away or so. Not at all a bad commute."

"He's actually moving to Atlanta in a few weeks, and even if he wasn't... I can't." She poured everything out from high school to now. She'd never told anyone but her therapist and Colt, but she needed to get it off her chest; it was crushing her.

"Is that why you never go to dinner with me or anywhere for social occasions? You're holding me at arm's length?" Susan turned on her blinker.

"It's nothing personal." It was the way it had to be to avoid triggers and lead a semi-calm life.

"It feels personal, Georgia. I love you like a sister, and I've been worried this entire time about everything happening to you. I knew you could have been…killed. But being your friend is worth the risk. So the question is would you rather—"

Georgia groaned. "Another Would You Rather question? Really?"

"Hear me out," Susan said through a chuckle. "Would you rather go your whole life never experiencing the love of someone and returning that love *or* loving and *losing* someone but having those memories to cherish forever?"

To love and lose or never love and be alone. She had loved and lost. And she often thought of those few years with Colt—the laughter, kisses, conversation. The way it made her feel full and satisfied. Sometimes when applying lotion, she'd remember how her hand fit perfectly in his. Or when she walked into a building she'd remember how he always opened doors for her. Even his merciless teasing she thought about with fondness.

Those memories were warm. Until they faded and she was left with the reminder that she was going to grow old alone—but with managed anxiety levels.

"I don't know," she said weakly.

"Do you think God wants you to be alone and afraid to have relationships? I'm not talking about people who feel called to be single in order to serve God—the kind the apostle Paul talks about. I'm talking about a woman who is clearly in love with a man who is obviously head over heels for her—but she pushes it away out of fear of things that may not ever happen. A woman too afraid to live. That kind of fear is not of God."

No, it wasn't. But she didn't know how else to move forward. "He's in law enforcement. Every day I'll make myself sick wondering if he's okay and he'll get tired of it. It'll be high school 2.0."

"Georgia, since you've been seeing a therapist and learning coping techniques, how far have you come on a one-to-ten scale?" She turned onto Amber's road.

"Six, maybe? Every day is different but I manage to make it through." God's grace had been sufficient. Every day. Every moment.

"Someone has tried to literally murder you for days, and here you are hard-pressed but not crushed. Struck down but not destroyed. Your faith is firmly planted in the Lord, and you haven't hidden under a rock and refused to come out. You have coping skills you didn't have fifteen years ago. It's about taking those negative thoughts captive and saying, 'God, here they are. Take them and make them bend under Your will. Remove and replace them with what truly belongs in my mind.'"

"Anyone ever tell you that you give good advice?"

Susan smirked. "Yes, all the time."

Georgia laughed as they pulled into Amber's drive. "I'll think about it. Besides, Colt is moving to Atlanta. My job is here, and come January I'll be editor in chief. I've wanted that for so long, and I don't see it happening in Atlanta."

"Maybe God has other dreams for you that aren't so safe as a small-town editor in chief—not that anything is wrong with that—but for you, again, it's safe."

Georgia leashed her dogs, and they bounded out of Susan's vehicle.

"I'll call you later."

"One last one. Would you rather stay in a safe bubble

or burst it and follow the love of your life into an uncertain and unknown place but be loved and cherished?" She waved. "Think on that!" She didn't give Georgia time to answer.

To be loved by Colt. Wake up with him, go to sleep at night next to him. Walk the dogs, have children. Children who might lose a father at a young age. Her stomach churned. But this wasn't living. Susan was right. She was walking dead.

Georgia knocked on Amber's door, and she opened it. Wyatt and Doc barked their greetings. She unleashed them inside, and Amber laughed. "Man, I love those dogs."

"Me too."

Georgia heard Gerald greet the dogs and chuckle. He came through the kitchen with a grin. "If Karen wasn't allergic, I'd have a few of my own. Colt called us. Told us about the coach and Terry Helms. We should have come clean about Jared taking the bribe, but we were all ashamed, and once he died, we wanted to bury it along with him. But one of them killed my son. I wonder if I'd said anything years ago if it would have helped."

"We all made mistakes, Dad." Amber rubbed his back.

"And everyone deserves grace," Georgia added.

"I guess you're right." He hefted a box that was stacked in Amber's living room. "I'll go load this with the others." He slipped out the front door.

"The church is doing a community yard sale, and I have a lot of things to let go of, including guilt. Thanks for being a friend and not berating me for my idiocy." She sat on the couch, and Wyatt jumped in her lap.

Gerald entered and rubbed his lower back. "You giving away gold, Amber?"

"Ha! I wish I had enough to give away gold." She turned to Georgia. "Did you see what was on the SD card?"

"No." Georgia sat in the recliner and rubbed Doc's head. "But one of Colt's agents is getting something so they can look at it. If for some reason Terry or Coach didn't kill Jared, I'm hoping whatever is on that SD card will lead them to the killer. I imagine it'll lead to Alice or Wade."

"You don't think it was Coach or Terry? We do."

"I don't know. Terry copped to fraud knowing he'd lose his job and even do some time. Coach admitted to Dandy and myself and even Harry. Who else is there?" Unless Chance was lying, or Scott. Or even Sunny Wilkerson. "We still don't know why Alice had her prints on Jared's watch. Says she didn't remember seeing him that night when she clearly did. She's hiding something, and I think it might be Wade's drug habit at the time."

"Well, at least you're safe now," Amber said.

Colt had Duncan Flanigan in one room writing out his statement and Terry Helms writing his in another room. Cody Weinbeck approached. What a tool. "Nice work, McCoy. Course, our season is shot, and homecoming is next Friday night."

"Yes, because sports is what's important over justice being served. You are a deputy, you know." He refrained from the eye roll.

"Maybe I like the power," he shot back and laughed. "I'm clocking out. I assume you're leaving town now that it's all wrapped up nice with a bow for you."

Except it wasn't. He wasn't technically here to find out who hurt Georgia but who killed Jared, and at this second, he wasn't sure. No one had come forward. "Depends on the statements." No point in prolonging his goodbye to Georgia, though. She didn't need to feel obligated to stick around now that she was finally able to be free of him.

"Seems to me one of those two did it." Cody shrugged and swaggered down the hall.

Mae rounded the corner with a frown.

"What's wrong? Couldn't find a device we can plug that SD into?" Colt asked.

"No, I got a computer. I just don't like that deputy."

Mae didn't like any man, let alone trust one, but she knew how to be a team player, and they worked well together. But the only personal things he knew about her were she liked unsweet tea and black coffee and had a soft spot for female victims. "Well, let's pop this bad boy in and see what we see."

She fired up the computer and inserted the SD card.

Rhett and Poppy rounded the corner, each with a paper in hand. "We got statements," Poppy said, "but you ain't gonna like it."

"Why?" Colt took Terry's statement. The loan fraud and illegal recruiting were admitted, but nothing about Jared. He then read Coach's and read it again. "He admits to every murder, break-in and attack—even poisoning the dogs—but there's nothing here about killing Jared or about cutting the brake lines and releasing the steering fluid. And I seriously doubt he'd forget doing that. Georgia shot one off to scare him away, and looking at my face—and hers—ought to do it."

"I'll go back in there and jog his memory. His lawyer is here, and of course it's Reggie Leeway. I do not like him." Poppy snarled.

No one did. He was making money off all this illegal activity by defending these people, except for Scott Hazer, whom he was representing pro bono to keep quiet about Chance's drug use—which Colt suspected was still going on presently. Poppy strode from the room while Colt, Mae and Rhett pulled up the photos. Some were photos of Jared's friends and football practice.

Then he got to the ones Jared had taken of Scott Hazer. There he was, clear as a bell, with Wade Parker—Alice's son.

"This might be why Alice didn't mention seeing Jared," Colt said. "She didn't want it to come out they'd talked about her son and the drugs." It would explain the print on his watch—if she'd grabbed him to keep him from leaving without promising to keep silent.

"If you can't get her to confess, we got nothing but circumstantial evidence." Mae shook her head.

If Alice was indeed the killer he suspected her to be. "I need to call Georgia. Update her." Or text her. Hearing her voice was too hard right now, but she needed to know where the case stood.

THIRTEEN

Georgia had gone through the last two boxes of Amber's clothes, since she had absolutely nothing. She'd grabbed a few T-shirts, jeans and an old pair of tennis shoes. She needed to do some shopping, since she'd only been able to grab a few necessities. She folded the box sides back together so Gerald could haul them out easier. Her phone chirped with a text.

She read it and gaped.

"What is it?" Amber asked.

"They saw the SD card. Scott was dealing to Wade Parker. Colt believes Alice may be Jared's killer, but she's not at work or home." Georgia texted she was at Amber's.

Colt texted back.

Come to station. There's more.

"I need to go to the sheriff's office," Georgia said. "There's more, and I'm afraid he didn't say, so it must be confidential and important."

"I can give you a lift. I'm on my way to the church," Gerald said.

Georgia hated to leave her dogs, since she'd only just

gotten them back. "Do you mind watching them while I go?" she asked Amber. "It might be a few hours depending on the news."

"Sure."

After loving on the dogs, she hauled herself into Gerald's truck. "You never drive the same vehicle. Nice perk of owning a dealership, huh?" she teased and clicked her seat belt in place.

He laughed. "I reckon so. It came on the lot last week, and I couldn't stand it. Had to have it myself."

"I hear ya." She couldn't get Alice out of her head. "Do you think Alice could have killed Jared, Gerald? I mean, if she did, I think it would have been an accident, and then there's the moving of his body. She isn't strong enough to do that. But Wade would have been. Or maybe Wade killed him, panicked and told his mom and they cleaned it up together. Colt sent Florida PD over to talk to him, but he wasn't home. They're hunting him down."

Gerald shook his head. "I don't know if I can believe Alice murdered Jared. Maybe Wade if he was using drugs." He glanced at his phone and groaned. "Hey, do you mind if we run by the dealership real quick? I got an issue. Won't take long."

"No, that's fine." She pulled out her phone to let Colt know she was with Gerald and it would be a few minutes longer before she arrived.

"Georgia, I'm gonna need you to put that phone back in your purse."

"What?" She glanced up to see a gun pointed right at her. Her pulse spiked and she froze.

"Phone. Back in your purse. Now. I can't have you telling the McCoy boy where you are. I need time..."

Time for what? What was happening? She carefully

put her phone back in her purse as her heart thundered against her ribs. "I don't understand."

Sweat poured down the sides of his beet-red cheeks. "It was an accident."

Alice had killed Jared and *Gerald* had helped her move the body?

"I made a lot of bad investments, and Karen was keeping the dealership afloat with her own money."

Probably money from life insurance from her first husband.

"When Jared was approached, I needed that ten thousand dollars, and I pushed him to take it so that I didn't have to use Karen's money, and really Ole Magnolia's not a bad school. The money would've helped me out and our family. Jared agreed. He kept a thousand dollars and the tickets, and I used the rest. When he told me that he wasn't going to go and we needed to give the money back...I was angry."

He. Was. Angry. "You killed him for that?"

Gerald kept the gun on her, glancing at the road and back to her, repeating the action. If she could get the gun while he was looking at the road, she might be able to save herself. Why kill her?

"No. I was angry, and I'd spent the money on bills and credit card debt. I didn't have it to give back. I thought I'd talk about it again with him. Or I'd have to tell Karen. She would have been disappointed, but she would have paid the money back."

"What happened?" she whispered.

"That night when he took the photos of Scott at the motel, he saw something he shouldn't have." Gerald's voice cracked. "Alice was a mistake. I tried to tell him it wouldn't ever happen again, but he was furious and he threatened to tell…" Panic, desperation and hysteria laced his voice.

The print on the watch. Not telling she'd seen Jared. It wasn't about Wade. She might never have known that Wade was in a room nearby buying drugs at the same time. It was about Gerald and Alice. "He threatened to tell Karen that he'd caught you and Alice having an affair."

"Yes," he cried. "He saw us coming out of the motel room, and when Alice left, he approached me. We argued, and he stormed off. I called Alice and told her. When she saw him at Rascal's, she tried to talk to him privately when he went to the restroom and wasn't with Chance. I imagine that's how her print ended up on his watch. When I heard that it was hers, I panicked. I can't let Karen know this! I'll lose her and the business and everything!"

"You killed her son. How have you looked her in the eyes all these years?"

Gerald wailed. "I'm not sure I have. I've been paying every day. Me and Alice stopped it that night. Never ever met up again. She quit the dealership, and we don't even so much as speak. We've changed."

"It doesn't change what you did, Gerald." She rubbed her temples. "What do you want with me? Colt has the SD card. Are you on it, too?"

"No! But two of my dealership cars probably are. Jared was parked right behind us. I knew if Colt got that SD card he'd put two and two together—especially having Alice's print. I tried to get it, but—"

Georgia's brain wouldn't slow down. So many thoughts. The terror. The tragedy. "Wait. You tried to get what? The

SD card?" It was him. He knew they were looking for it, and he must have overheard Amber call them to meet her at work for it. So he showed up, and while they were in the stables, he messed with Colt's truck with hopes of them dying in a car accident or at least being knocked out long enough for him to steal the SD card. Then it would go back to a cold case that couldn't be solved. Alice's prints would mean nothing without evidence that she hurt Jared.

He turned into the dealership parking lot. By now it was closed for the night. Empty. No one to run to.

"Why did you move the body? Where did you kill him?"

Gerald's face fell, and he motioned her to slide out on his side. "I called him to talk about it. He was at the training room."

That was the quick call from him to Jared that night. It didn't need to be a long call. Jared would know exactly what Gerald wanted to talk about.

"He met me here. It escalated. He was telling Karen about the affair and the money that I'd spent as well as giving back the tickets. Nothing I said changed his mind. I couldn't—I just—I hit him with a paperweight that had been lying on my desk."

Oh, Jared.

"I didn't mean to kill him. But he stopped moving and I panicked." He jammed the gun into her back and marched her in the side entrance to his office.

He'd moved Jared to keep from incriminating himself, and no one even looked at him because he was the only dad Jared knew. He barely remembered his real dad. The gun poked her side and she winced, already sore from the car wreck.

"What are you going to do with me?" she asked again. The fact he wasn't answering that question terrified her.

Gerald wiped his nose on his sleeve. "I have no choice now. Since I couldn't get the card, I've got to get out of town. Leave the country. I'm not going to prison, and I can't face Karen. So you, Georgia, are the leverage I need to ensure I get out safely."

She'd gone from armchair detective to hostage in a matter of days.

"I'm going to give you the combination to this safe, and you're going to open it for me to get some cash and I'm getting out of town."

Would he kill her? Was there a point?

Didn't matter. He wasn't thinking rationally or logically. He'd never make it out alive. But maybe that's what he wanted—to die instead of facing his fears. Of prison. Of Karen despising him.

Fears had to be faced.

But she wasn't facing hers. With shaky fingers, she knelt in his office and looked up at Gerald.

"Five."

She pressed the five button.

"Six. One. Six. Eight."

The door clicked.

"Open it and put the cash in this bag." He placed a backpack on the chair next to the safe. Inside the safe was a wad of cash. Several thousand dollars.

"Now what?" She was afraid of the answer.

Gerald's glance darted from one window to the other and then around the room to the cash. His breath came in gasps and pants as moisture leaked down his face like rivulets of rain on a window pane. Oh, yeah. The signs were obvious. She'd lived with them most of her life.

Panic.

One did not make rational or good choices in this state. But one thing she knew thanks to Celeste…coping skills.

"Gerald, you're having a panic attack. I understand. You need to breathe." Not that she wanted to help him, but helping him helped herself. "Deep breath in. And out."

He wasn't listening. A million horrific scenes and thoughts were playing out in his head. Growing worse and more dramatic. Been there, done that.

Somehow, she wasn't panicking. Fear coursed through her. An unpredictable man with a gun was panicking. But there was a calm washing over her she couldn't explain, other than the peace of God. He was with her. Through this.

"Listen to me," she said softly. "You have to calm down. Breathe."

Finally he made solid eye contact and listened and breathed. She walked him through inhales and exhales. "You've been through a lot and you've made a mess, but don't make it worse. You need to let me go and turn yourself in."

"I can't. I—I won't! Get up!"

So much for trying to make him see reason, but he had more of his faculties and he wasn't as shaky; hopefully that sliver of control would keep her alive.

She rose slowly.

"Give me the bag."

Georgia carefully handed him the backpack, and he slung it around his shoulder; the gun continued to stare her down. Gerald had killed Jared and attempted to murder her and Colt. Who was to say he wouldn't kill her now?

Georgia had been so afraid of triggers she'd opted out of growing close to anyone and refused to allow herself the freedom to love Colt. She'd flat-out rejected him. Now she was literally staring down a trigger that could cut her off from everything.

Susan's Would You Rather question looped through her brain, and right here as she fought for her life, all she could think about was Colt and yes, yes, it would be worth it to love him. And if the worst did happen, at least she would carry cherished memories of their love.

And he was willing to risk loving her, and who knew what tomorrow might bring to her? He'd be left to grieve her, but she was worth it to him. Love…love was worth it. Love was living. Taking risks and trusting God with each moment. Believing in Him to guide them and get them through for better or worse. She'd been so stupid. Letting fear control and dictate her life.

Now she might never even get the chance to reveal to Colt how she felt. That she was willing if he would give her a third chance. If she hadn't hurt him past the point of forgiveness. Could she remind him forgiveness was a thing again and change his mind?

Could she live through this?

"Out the door. Now."

"Where are we going?" she asked as she obeyed his commands and waited for an opportunity to make a break for it.

"I don't know. I have to get out of town, and you're my insurance that I get out unharmed." He nudged her with the gun and forced her outside and toward the truck.

How far would he take this? Take her?

And when he realized it was a fruitless effort, would he dispose of her?

* * *

Colt had never experienced the kind of anxiety and panic Georgia talked of until now. Now he was displaying every symptom, and he could not make his mind shut down as thoughts of a dead Georgia played out on a constant loop in his mind.

Use her tactics. *What evidence do you have to support the thought she might die?* She is with a killer who has tried to murder her already. *What's the worst that could happen?* She could die! *Can you live with that?*

Emphatically no!

He raced the SUV toward the only place Gerald might go. Once he'd seen the SD card, a deputy had hauled in Alice. While that was going down, he'd noticed the two vehicles from Wilcox's dealership parked next to one another in the images, and the dots then connected.

When Alice was brought in, she'd admitted to an affair with Gerald and to Jared discovering it. She also came clean about the print. That night at Rascal's she caught him coming out of the restroom and grabbed him to plead for him to stay quiet. It was over. It would never happen again. She immediately quit when Gerald told her Jared knew. They'd never ever seen one another romantically again. She'd gotten things right with the Lord and sought forgiveness.

She had no clue Wade had been doing drugs or that there was a photo, only that Jared had seen her and Gerald at the motel. She never once thought Gerald had killed Jared—but the circumstantial evidence pointed to him—but that had been a tragedy and an opportunity for her to get things right in her marriage and with God.

The Florida police spoke with Wade, who admitted to buying weed, but he had no idea Jared had taken photos and was mortified. He'd been a dumb kid rebelling because his parents were fighting a lot at that time, but after Jared's death things turned around in their family, and when he went to college, he stopped all the partying.

Neither Terry nor Coach admitted to cutting Colt's brake lines and releasing steering fluid. Georgia didn't end up at the station. Amber had said Gerald had given her a ride on his way to the church—in his big-engine Denali truck. A phone call to the church had let him know that Gerald had never arrived, and Georgia wasn't answering her phone. The only place he knew to look was the dealership.

He hadn't thought, just ran out of the station to find her.

Weaving through vehicles on the road, he spotted Gerald's truck up ahead in the parking lot. He whipped into the lot and bounded out of the car in time to see Gerald grab Georgia around the throat and put the gun to her head.

"Whoa," Colt said, keeping his distance and slowly raising his hands to show he was unarmed. "Let's keep calm, Gerald. You don't want to hurt Georgia. You've known her most of her life. She's Amber's closest friend. Let's just talk—you and me." His pulse pounded in his throat, and he could barely swallow.

"What's there to say? You know what I did."

"I don't. I don't know. All I've been told is you and Alice had an affair and Jared found out. He confronted you."

Gerald broke into sobs, but he didn't lower his weapon. His emotional state made him careless, and all Colt could think about was him pulling that trigger and ending everything good that had ever been a part of

Colt's life. The only woman he'd loved who had made him feel special.

And yes, brought him considerable pain, but it didn't matter. Not in this moment; he'd risk her rejection a hundred times over.

"We can work it out."

"How?" Gerald bellowed. "I killed Jared and Karen will never forgive me. Never love me. Amber will hate me. I can't go to prison. My only chance is getting out of here, and she's going with me to make sure I get out unharmed."

Colt took one step closer. "Gerald," he said softly, "I want to help you. Yes, you've made a big mess. Yes, you've hurt your family—but it's possible in time they'll forgive you. You have to be a man now and accept the consequences for your actions. You. Alice. Everyone who's kept secrets. The love of my life once told me—" he looked at Georgia—"right into her wide-with-fright eyes "—told me forgiveness is a thing, and she's right."

Gerald squeezed tighter around Georgia's neck. "Not this. This can never be forgiven."

"Everything can be forgiven—in time. But I'm gonna be real honest here with ya, Gerald. If you don't let her go, I'm gonna have to take drastic measures." He wasn't even close to playing the hostage-negotiator angle well, but Gerald wasn't a bad man. He'd done a lot of bad things to cover up other bad things. "Do you understand? What if someone had a gun to Karen or Amber? Would you let him take them?"

Gerald's hand shook, and he looked at Georgia. She trembled and her tears had streaked her face, but she was breathing deep and keeping control.

"No—no, I wouldn't."

"Right. Drop the gun. Be reasonable. It's over, Gerald. There's nowhere to go. They'll find you at the state line, at the airport. All you're going to do is hurt more people. Drop the gun."

Gerald slowly removed his grip from Georgia and dropped the weapon. She raced toward Colt and into his arms, but he didn't have time to hold her or kiss her or anything. He cuffed Gerald, retrieved the weapon and called in backup and his team.

Then he grabbed Georgia into his arms, and she hung on like he might let her go. That was one thing he didn't want to do. Not ever.

She looked up into his eyes as the sirens sounded in the distance. "I'm sorry. I made a mistake. Twice. But I won't make it again."

Did she mean what he thought she did? "What about your trigger?"

"Susan also hit me upside the head with a metaphorical volleyball today."

He grinned. "Hurts, don't it?"

"Not as much as saying goodbye to you did today. But then… I hear you have a love of your life. Who is this woman? You never mentioned her."

The woman had the nerve to tease him at a moment like this. "Real funny."

"I've learned to cope. I will cope."

"I'll quit."

"No, you will not. You were born for this job. I'm proud of you." Those words. They meant more than anything to him.

"I love you, Georgia." He descended upon her lips,

kissing her in a way that clearly identified how much he loved her, needed her and wanted to be with her. Whatever the cost.

FOURTEEN

Georgia sat in a lawn chair on her property while the dogs ran and played. Colt sat next to her with a glass of sweet tea as they looked on the house they were building. It had been six months since Gerald had been arrested for Jared's murder and the attempted murder of her and Colt. He would be going to prison. As of yet, Karen hadn't forgiven him—maybe never would. Amber had only seen him twice.

The town had been turned upside down with the news of illegal recruiting. Courage High lost their coach and their secretary, who had let the proof of residence slide as a favor to Terry—and a small loan she didn't have the credit to receive. Coach would be going to prison. Terry lost his job and was going to have to face charges for fraud, but his wife had stuck by him. However, their house went on the market two weeks after everything went public.

Georgia offered to leave Magnolia and go with Colt to Atlanta, but he'd decided to move back here and keep his job with the cold case unit. He was only moving to prove his worth; he said his job didn't prove anything about who he was as a person and finally knowing that made it easy to keep his position at the MBI, which he loved. The commute was only forty minutes.

Loving him was worth the risk. In two more months, they were having a June wedding right here on the property. Their house would be done. And they'd get their life together.

"What are you over there thinking about?" Colt asked and took her hands, hauling her to her feet. "Work?" Charlie had made good, and in January Georgia had taken over as editor in chief. Removed the horrible navy curtains and established an online paper and was in the works with a developer from Honeyhaven—a town not too far away—for a *Magnolia Gazette* app.

God hadn't delivered her from her anxiety. She might always battle it. Might always take some meds to help. But she was okay with that. Her faith in God was strong, and He'd proven that while He may not remove her from the battle, He was walking her through it each and every moment—and some days carrying her. His grace was sufficient for her. Didn't mean she stopped praying for complete healing, but she was confident that whatever happened, she could get through it if she leaned into Him.

"No, I'm not thinking about work. I'm thinking how glad I am we're together." She glanced at her carat solitaire in a thick gold band and grinned. She could have missed out on so many good things—like love and a life with Colt—if she'd been too afraid to even take a chance.

But she prayed daily, and she'd acquired some good coping skills and healthy replacement thoughts.

He brushed a strand of hair from her eyes. "I am, too. We'll get through the bouts of anxiety together. You and me, Georgia Jane—we're a team. In this together."

Her insides puddled. "You know it also helps when you kiss me. Chases away all my worrisome thoughts."

She grinned teasingly as he met her lips, kissing her expertly, with finesse, and languidly, as if the world would wait on them, then softly pecked her brow, her nose, then met her lips, whispering against them, "Well, I guess we'll have to never stop kissing. Can you live with that?"

What's the worst that could happen? She could lose her breath and go out in total utter bliss? "Oh, yeah. I can live with that."

* * * * *

*If you like cold case stories,
pick up one of Jessica R. Patch's previous books,*
Cold Case Christmas

Available now from Love Inspired Suspense.

Dear Reader,

Maybe like Georgia, you too are riddled with anxiety, wondering if God is ever going to "fix" it. Like Georgia, it may be something you battle on a daily or hourly basis, but I hope you see how much God is for you, and how much grace He will give you to get through the tough moments. And if you don't suffer from anxiety or panic disorder, I hope you've learned like Colt how to extend grace and be understanding of someone who does. My sister, Celeste, is a counselor, and she helped me by offering me the coping questions that she gives to her clients. I used them for Georgia in the story. Maybe they'll help you, too.

I love to connect with readers. Please visit my website and sign up for my newsletter at *www.jessicarpatch.com*, and follow me on BookBub! *https://www.bookbub.com/profile/jessica-r-patch*.

Jessica

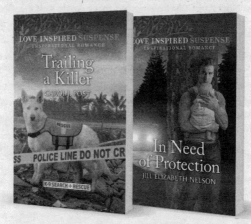